"This is the perfect solution."

"Mr. Papadakis, living with you is the last thing I want. Ben and I are happy as we are. I love my little house. Why should I give it up? And for that matter, where's your wife? Why can't she bring up her own child?"

Andreas's eyes shadowed as his thoughts raced back to the blackest days of his life. "My wife's dead," he told her bluntly. "And you wouldn't need to give up your house— you could let it." He saw the uncertainty in her eyes and pressed home his faint advantage. "Sit down. Think again about the benefits."

MARGARET MAYO was reading Mills & Boon romances long before she began to write them. In fact she never had any plans to become a writer. After an idea for a short story popped into her head she was thrilled when it turned into a full-scale novel. Now, over twenty-five years later she is still happily writing and says she has no intention of stopping.

She lives with her husband Ken in a rural part of Staffordshire, England. She has two children, Adrian, who now lives in America, and Tina. Margaret's hobbies are reading, photography and more recently water-colour painting, which she says has honed her observational skills and is a definite advantage when it comes to writing.

The MEDITERRANEAN TYCOON

MARGARET MAYO

MEDITERRANEAN PASSIONS

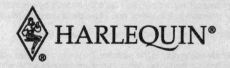

HARLEQUIN®

TORONTO • NEW YORK • LONDON
AMSTERDAM • PARIS • SYDNEY • HAMBURG
STOCKHOLM • ATHENS • TOKYO • MILAN • MADRID
PRAGUE • WARSAW • BUDAPEST • AUCKLAND

ISBN 0-373-80615-9

THE MEDITERRANEAN TYCOON

First North American Publication 2003.

CHAPTER ONE

PETA'S chin had a determined thrust as she knocked on the door. Many tales had travelled around the company about the dynamic new owner. He was the literal clean-sweeping new broom.

Already, in the space of a few weeks, many employees had left; no one wanted to work for the Tyrant, as he'd promptly been nicknamed. And now she had been promoted to his personal assistant. His third one in as many weeks! He hadn't asked whether she would like the job, oh, no. A directive had been sent to her. It implicated that she either take the job or leave the company.

It had put Peta's back up. She had disliked him immediately and intensely, but the fact was that she needed the job and couldn't afford to turn it down.

'Come!'

The voice was deep and resonant. She'd seen Andreas Papadakis when he'd stalked the corridors of Linam Shipping, when he'd swept through the offices, dark eyes seeing all. They'd rested on each employee in turn, reading and assessing, causing several of her female associates to swoon.

Peta had seen only a tall, arrogant man, who would have been handsome if his face wasn't creased into a permanent scowl. He'd projected a tough, invincible image, and she hadn't been impressed. She liked men with humanity and warmth. This man certainly hadn't the right disposition to warm himself to his employees. He was simply here to turn an already profitable company into a much bigger money-spinner.

She took a steadying breath before opening the door, her back ramrod-straight as she walked across the oatmeal carpet towards the huge, dominating desk. It was the first time she'd been in this holy sanctum and the oak panelling, the original oil paintings and the antique furniture were very impressive, though she somehow guessed they weren't what this man would have chosen for himself. He'd already installed a whole bank of computers and other high-tech office equipment, and they sat uneasily in what had once been old Mr Brown's office.

Andreas Papadakis stood to one side of the fine desk, his hair brushed uncompromisingly back, black brows beetled together, brown eyes narrowed and assessing. He looked the very picture of intimidation and Peta squared her shoulders. 'Good morning, Mr Papadakis,' she said evenly.

'Miss James.' He inclined his head. 'Sit down—please.' The please seemed to be an afterthought as he indicated the chair in front of his desk.

Peta sat, then wished she hadn't when he remained standing. He had to be at least six foot four, broad-shouldered and powerfully muscled, and those rich chestnut eyes watched every movement she made, making her feel distinctly uncomfortable.

Not that she let it show. She lifted her chin and fixed a bright smile to her lips, pencil poised above her notebook.

The rest of the day passed in a whirlwind of note-taking and meetings, of barked orders, of booking appointments and sending dozens of e-mails. Peta's opinion of Andreas Papadakis didn't change one iota; if anything she thought him even more arrogant and overbearing. But she nevertheless felt quite pleased with the way she had handled herself, sure that she'd passed her induction with flying colours, and was on the verge of putting on her jacket when her new employer flung open the connecting door between their two offices.

'Not so fast, Miss James. There's still work to be done.'

Peta glanced at the clock on the wall. 'I thought my hours were nine till five,' she said, her wide blue eyes fixed challengingly on his. 'It's already two minutes past.' Adding beneath her breath, And if you think I'm going to work late you have another think coming. I have a home life even if you don't.

'I couldn't care less if it's twenty past,' he lashed out. 'I need you.'

If this was the way he'd spoken to his previous secretaries then it was no wonder they'd walked out, decided Peta. What was wrong with asking politely instead of yelling and demanding? Unfortunately, if she wanted to keep the job, it looked as though it was a case of holding the candle to the devil.

'Very well,' she answered calmly, while seething inside as she hung up her jacket again. 'What is it you want me to do? I've finished all the work.'

He threw a tape down on her desk. 'I want this report by six. Make sure you type the figures correctly; it's very important.'

I bet it is, Peta said to herself, as soon as he'd closed the dividing door between them. Everything is important, according to you. She'd tied her thick auburn hair back this morning, but during the course of the day it had come loose and she tossed it back angrily now.

Picking up the phone, she called her neighbour. 'Marnie, I have to work late. Do you think you could look after Ben a while longer?' She hated having to leave her son a minute more than was necessary, felt guilty about it, even, but there was no way round it. Ben was very special to her. She wanted him to have the best possible start in life, and if that meant going out to work then that was what she had to do.

'Of course I will, love,' came the immediate reply. 'Don't worry about him. I'll give him his supper, shall I?'

Marnie loved looking after Ben. Her grandchildren were now teenagers and she missed having a small child around the house. She was a treasure. Peta didn't know what she'd do without her.

It was almost seven by the time she finally left the office. Andreas Papadakis was a workaholic and expected everyone else to be the same, heaping work on her that would surely have waited until the next day. She'd heard that some mornings he was at his desk by six.

She had no idea whether he was married or not. He didn't wear a ring and he protected his privacy fiercely, although all sorts of rumours floated around the company. Rumours of strings of attractive girlfriends, of a wife in Greece and a mistress in England, of properties in New York and the Bahamas, as well as in Europe and his homeland. How he had time for all this Peta wasn't sure.

When she arrived for work at ten minutes to nine the next morning he was waiting for her. 'I wondered when you were going to show up,' he muttered tersely, brown eyes glaring. His tie was hanging loose, top button undone, and his thick, straight hair looked as though he'd constantly raked agitated fingers through it. In fact he looked as though he'd spent the night in the office wrestling with insurmountable problems.

'I need coffee, strong and black, and half a dozen muffins. Blueberry. See to it, will you?'

The day had begun! Peta nodded. 'I could order you a proper breakfast if you'd—'

'Just do as I ask,' he cut in impatiently. 'And bring in your notebook. There's lots of work to get through.'

He was in a foul mood for the whole day but Peta stubbornly refused to give in, remaining pleasant, polite and helpful, no matter what harsh thoughts she entertained beneath the surface, and there were plenty of those.

By the end of the week she began to feel complacent; she felt that she now totally understood her employer and hopefully he was happy with her. His moods were legendary but Peta chose to ignore them—and on the whole it worked. It was not until he once more asked her to work late that it all began to go wrong.

'I'm sorry, I can't,' she said firmly. Why did he have to choose today of all days?

The famous frown dragged his brows together, beetling them over glittering chestnut eyes. 'I beg your pardon?'

'It's impossible for me to stay on today.'

'I presume you have a good reason?' he barked.

'Yes, I do as a matter of fact,' she announced, her chin just that little bit higher. 'It's my son's birthday.'

He looked thunderstruck. 'You have a son? Why the hell wasn't I told? You're no good to me if you're constantly taking time off.'

Peta's eyes flashed a deep, defensive blue. 'What do you mean, constantly? This is a special occasion, Mr Papadakis. Ben's eight today and he's having a party at McDonald's; I refuse to let him down. The only other occasion I couldn't work was when he had appendicitis. And even then I counted it as my holiday.'

She saw the flicker in his eyes, the faint doubt, then the grim nod. 'Very well. Can you manage a few hours in the morning?'

He was asking, not telling! A faint victory! It was Saturday tomorrow, and Ben's football practice. But under the circumstances Peta felt that it would be unwise to refuse him again. Marnie would take Ben; she'd love it. 'Yes, I can do that.'

'Good.' With a nod he dismissed her.

It never ceased to amaze Peta how good Andreas Papadakis's English was. He had scarcely the trace of an accent. If it hadn't been for his dark Hellenic looks she would have taken him for an Englishman any day. She could see why most girls in the office fancied him. What they hadn't experienced were his flashes of temper, his holier-than-thou attitude. It made you instantly forget how good-looking he was, how sexily he moved.

He was without a doubt a lethally attractive man— she had felt his physical presence many times; she'd have had to be made of ice not to—but in the main all she ever saw was the face of a tyrant. And she disliked him as much now as she had in the beginning. She found it hard to believe that he'd backed down over her working this evening.

'Mum, this is the best party ever,' Ben announced, munching his way through his second burger.

Peta grinned. The noise was deafening, every one of his eight friends talking at once, all happy and excited. To them this was a million times better than having a party at home with jelly and ice cream.

'And which one of you lucky young fellows is Ben?' asked a deep voice behind her. A familiar voice! Peta twisted in her chair, gasping in amazement when she saw Andreas Papadakis just a couple of feet away, a huge parcel tucked under one arm and an amazing twinkle in his eyes. He looked a very different man from the one she had left a couple of short hours ago.

'Mr Papadakis,' she gasped. 'What are you doing here?' She stood up then, felt her heart hammering a thousand beats a minute.

'I've brought a present for the birthday boy. Which one is he?'

By this time all eyes were on Ben, whose face had flushed with embarrassment. 'Who are you?' he asked, his chin jutting in the same way as his mother's. There was no mistaking their relationship. Although his hair was darker, he had the same wide-spaced blue eyes and an identical jawline.

'I'm your mother's employer. She told me it was your birthday. I thought you might like this.' And he handed Ben the giant parcel.

Peta was too shocked for words. This wasn't the same man. The Andreas Papadakis she worked for would never have thought about buying a birthday present for an employee's child, let alone personally delivering it.

'You're—very kind,' she murmured. 'You didn't have to do that.' There came the faint notion that perhaps he was checking on her, finding out for himself whether she'd been telling the truth when she said it was Ben's birthday, but no sooner had the thought flitted into her mind than she dismissed it as disloyal. She really didn't know the first thing about this man—except that he was the devil incarnate to work with.

'I can't stay,' he said now, 'I have other things to do.

Enjoy the party. I'll expect you at nine in the morning, Miss James.'

'Yes,' said Peta faintly. 'And thank you again.'

No one else noticed him leave, everyone was watching Ben open his parcel, and there was a collective 'Oooh!' when the colourful wrapping fell to the floor revealing a magnificent Scalextric set. And when the lid came off the box there was so much track and so many cars that Peta felt sure it would take up the whole floor area of Ben's bedroom and spill out onto the landing as well. It was every boy's dream.

Her first instinct was to say that he couldn't accept such an expensive gift and that he must give it back, but seeing the look of sheer pleasure and amazement on Ben's face made her think again. It wasn't as if Andreas Papadakis couldn't afford it.

Maybe it was a thank-you for all the hard work she'd put in. Or—her mouth twisted wryly—maybe it was a sweetener so that she wouldn't say no to him again when he asked her to work late! She couldn't really believe that her boss had a big enough heart to buy her son a present when he hadn't even met him. She wasn't even sure he had a heart. But whatever his reasons it had pleased Ben, and he was her main concern.

When she went in to work on Saturday morning she fully intended thanking Mr Papadakis again, but gone was the man of yesterday evening. He was in his head-of-the-firm mode and it brooked no personal conversation. Nevertheless when he stood over her, one hand on the back of her chair, one on the desk, watching the screen as she typed a letter he was waiting for, she was aware now that a warm human being existed behind that harsh exterior. And because of that she began to feel his primal sexuality, the sheer physical dynamics of the man.

'You've missed out a word.'

Peta silently groaned. She'd do more than that if he didn't move. He was wearing a musky sandalwood cologne that was essentially male and would remind her of him for evermore. It took a supreme amount of willpower to carry on typing the letter and she made more mistakes in that one page than she normally did in a whole day.

'What's wrong?' he asked sharply. 'Not got it together yet? Did the party tire you out?'

Hardly, when it had been finished by eight. Had he no idea that he was the one making her nervous? 'I'm all right,' she answered. 'And by the way, thank you again for buying Ben that Scalextric. It was much too expensive a present, but he's absolutely delighted with it. He had me up at six this morning helping him put it together.'

'Good, I'm glad he liked it. Bring the letter in to me when you've printed it. And I'd like Griff's report next.'

He strode away, clearly not interested in discussing Ben's party or his gift. And she'd thought he had a heart after all. How wrong could she have been?

The morning fled. No mention had been made of how long he wanted her to work, though Peta had assumed she'd finish about one. But one o'clock came and went and there was no sign of him letting up.

His voice came through the open doorway. 'Miss James, get some lunch sent in.'

Peta groaned inwardly; surely he wasn't expecting her to remain here all day?

Then he strode into her office. 'After that you'd better go home and spend some time with your boy.'

'Thank you,' she said, wondering at his sudden generosity. 'And if you don't mind me saying so, you work far too hard yourself. Mr Brown didn't used to do the hours you do.'

'That's why the company was running downhill fast,' he retorted.

'What do you mean, downhill?' Peta asked quickly. 'It was extremely successful.' She'd always counted herself lucky to be working for such a flourishing firm.

Andreas Papadakis shook his head. 'That's the impression he wanted you to have. He didn't want unhappy employees, but a few more months and you'd have all been out of work.'

She looked at him with a disbelieving frown. 'Is that true?'

'Of course it's damn well true. I bought a sinking ship, Miss James, it's what I do. But I sure as hell make sure they never capsize.'

Peta supposed she ought to have known from the content of his correspondence that there were problems, except that she'd thought he was simply sweeping clean all the old methods and installing new ones of his own. He'd drummed up an awful lot of new business as well. She had privately accused him of rubbing his hands at all the extra money he was generating, not realising for one second that if he hadn't she'd have lost her job. It looked as if she'd wrong-footed him every step of the way.

Only once in the days that followed did he ask her to work late. 'I appreciate that you want to spend time with your son,' he said, 'but this really is important.'

How could she refuse when he asked her like that? But when on Friday afternoon he said that he wanted her to attend a conference with him on the following Monday and that it would mean a very late night she looked at him sharply. 'I don't think I can do that.'

She had never in the whole of Ben's life let anyone else bath him and put him to bed. It was a pleasure she looked forward to. It was their special time of day; it eased the guilt of her leaving him while she went to work. Marnie would be in her element, and Ben would probably enjoy it too if the truth were know because he adored her as much as the older woman adored him, but Peta knew that she would feel truly awful.

In any case, what conference went on into the early hours? He had to be joking. 'I can't promise anything,' she said.

'Can't or won't?' he demanded, mouth grim all of a sudden. 'I can easily find someone to step into your job, Miss James.'

This was the first time in ages that she had seen a flash of his old self. She ought to have known that his understanding behaviour was too good to last. 'I doubt it,' she replied, adding with great daring, 'No one else has been able to put up with your impossible demands.'

Fierce black brows jutted over narrowed eyes. 'Is that why you think my other PAs left?'

She nodded. 'It's what everyone believes.'

He perched himself on the edge of her desk, too near for comfort, causing an alarming flurry of her senses. They were becoming too frequent for her own good. She was joining the others, seeing him as a sexually exciting male instead of an impossible boss.

'Then I think I should put the matter straight,' he announced. 'They didn't leave because they couldn't work with me. I fired them because of their inadequacies.'

Peta shot him a flashing blue glance. 'Maybe what

you call inadequacies and what we girls consider to be unfair requests are two different things.'

His eyes narrowed still further until they were no more than two glittering slits. 'I think I've been more than reasonable, but if you think it unfair that I occasionally ask you to work extra hours, for which I might add you are handsomely paid, then I suggest you put your coat on and walk, too.'

Peta couldn't believe she had landed herself in this situation. She really oughtn't to have spoken to him like that. He was her employer after all. 'It's all right, I'll do it,' she said hastily.

'Good,' he clipped, and returned to his office.

She was walking out through the door at the end of the day, her thoughts already running ahead to her darling son and how she could make it up to him, when Andreas Papadakis's voice arrested her.

'The conference starts at two on Monday. Wear your smartest suit, Miss James, and it might be advisable to pack a cocktail dress for the evening.'

Warning bells rang in her head. She lurched round and stared at him. 'A cocktail dress?'

'That's right.'

Something was seriously wrong here, she decided as she headed towards her car. It sounded as though he needed a partner, not a personal assistant. And she wasn't sure that she wanted to be that person. The trouble was she had already promised.

CHAPTER TWO

ON SUNDAY afternoon Peta took Ben to the park to feed the ducks. She'd wound down from her hard week at work and was feeling happy and relaxed, enjoying Ben's company—until, on their return, she saw Andreas Papadakis's sleek black Mercedes parked outside her cottage. Her heart-rate increased a thousandfold and she couldn't even begin to think why he was here.

'Wow!' exclaimed her son. 'Whose is that?'

There was no time to answer because, as they approached, her employer levered his long frame out of the car and leaned nonchalantly against it, arms folded, legs crossed, a faint smile softening his all-too-often austere features. His casual pose emphasised his dynamic sexuality and Peta felt a tightening of her muscles. Her smile in response was little more than a grimace.

It was the first time she'd seen him in anything other than a collar and tie. In a blue thin-knit half-sleeved shirt, grey chinos and loafers he looked far less formidable. But infinitely more dangerous! She was scared of the sensations he managed to arouse in her these days.

Ben broke the awkward silence. 'You're my mummy's boss, aren't you? Thank you for my Scalextric; I love it. Me and Mummy put it together. Would you like to come and play?'

Andreas Papadakis smiled briefly. 'Some other time, perhaps. I need to talk to your mother.'

Somehow Peta couldn't see this indomitable man getting down on his knees and playing racing cars with an

17

eight-year-old boy. 'Mr Papadakis is here on business, Ben. He hasn't time to play,' she consoled him, at the same time wondering exactly why he had come calling.

She unlocked the door and Ben ran straight up to his room, and as her boss was standing right behind her she had no alternative but to invite him in, even though she would have preferred to talk outside.

It wasn't really a cottage, although it went under that name. It was a small, old town house on the outskirts of Southampton. She would have liked something grander but it was all she could afford, and it was home. It was clean and tidy and the furniture she'd renovated suited the house. She was happy here.

In her sitting room she turned to face him. 'This is quite a surprise, Mr Papadakis. Is the conference off tomorrow? Is that what you've come to tell me?'

'No, indeed,' he stated emphatically. 'I simply wanted to make sure that you'd come prepared. You looked somewhat shocked when I suggested a cocktail dress.'

'I was,' she claimed. 'I still am. You make it sound as though we're going to a party. And I—'

'It's no party, I assure you,' he interjected swiftly.

'Then why the cocktail dress?' She wondered whether she ought to suggest he sit down. But no, he might stay too long, and that was the last thing she wanted.

'Because after the conference we're having dinner,' he explained with exaggerated patience. 'Naturally we'll go on talking business, but it's not the sort of place where you can underdress.'

Peta narrowed her eyes speculatively, her head tilted to one side. 'And in what exact capacity would I be going?' It was something she needed to get very clear in her mind right from the beginning.

Eyebrows rose. 'Why, as my very able assistant. I

thought you understood that. I shall rely on you to take notes, make sure I didn't miss anything. You can familiarise yourself with the agenda in the morning. As I said, the conference begins at two. We'll have a sandwich lunch in the office.' He paused and studied her face intently. 'You still don't look as though you're sure about coming.'

'I somehow don't think I have a choice.'

'Correct. It's all part of the job. Is it your son you're worried about? Have you no one to look after him?'

'I have, yes, but he's my whole life, I hate leaving him. I feel I'm letting him down.'

He nodded as if he understood, but she couldn't see how, and when he turned towards the door she gave a sigh of relief. 'I'll see you at nine sharp in the morning,' he said. 'Say goodbye to your son for me.'

'His name's Ben.'

'Say goodbye to Ben for me, then.'

'Why don't you do it yourself? He's dying for you to see his Scalextric in action.' Now, why had she said that when she was anxious to be rid of him? Peta gave a mental shake of her head. She was out of her mind.

Andreas shot a look at his watch. 'I really should be getting back, but—maybe a couple of minutes.'

Back to whom? wondered Peta as she led him up the stairs. His current girlfriend? His mistress? Or back to the office? Did he work on a Sunday?

She felt his eyes boring into her back, maybe assessing her figure, her bottom in her tight denim jeans, checking her out to see whether she could be added to his list of conquests. Some chance!

But Ben had spotted them. 'Hello, have you come to play?' he asked brightly.

'Only to look,' explained Andreas. 'It's a very fine

layout you have there, but maybe if you…' In no time at all he was on his knees making adjustments, much to Peta's amazement, and it was another half-hour before he finally left.

Ben couldn't stop talking about him. 'Is that man going to come again?' he kept asking. 'Look what he did, Mummy. It's so much better. Come and play with me.'

But Peta had other more important things on her mind. 'Not now, darling, we have to go and see Auntie Susan.' Sue wasn't really Ben's aunt; she was a friend from her schooldays, divorced and happy, leading a full social life.

'Peta, how lovely to see you. And hello, Ben. How are you, little man? Come in, come in. I'll put the kettle on. Unless you'd like wine, Peta? You look worried. Is everything OK?'

'I've come to ask a favour. I need a cocktail dress for tomorrow night.'

Sue's brown eyes widened and her mouth broke into a smile. 'You've got a new boyfriend? Wonderful! Tell me about him. What's his name? How did you meet? Where—?'

'Shut up, Sue,' laughed Peta. 'It's nothing like that. It's a business do. I'm going with my boss.'

'The one you told me about? The Tyrant? Goodness, I bet you're not looking forward to that!'

Peta grimaced. 'It's either go or lose my job.'

Sue's eyes flashed. 'The man's a pig. Come on; let's have a look. We need to knock that man dead. Make him realise how irresistible you are. Hey, Ben, do you want the telly on while we go upstairs?'

'I don't want to be irresistible,' retorted Peta.

'Indispensable, then; you know what I mean,' said Sue airily. 'What sort of a do is it?'

'I don't altogether know,' said Peta, following her friend. 'A conference, followed by a black-tie dinner, but the meeting goes on while we eat, apparently.'

'Sounds fishy to me,' snorted Susan. 'Are you sure he hasn't got his eye on you?'

Peta laughed. Andreas Papadakis certainly had no designs on her, of that she was very sure.

At work the next morning her employer gave her no time to think about what lay ahead. It was head down and get on with it. They hardly had time to eat the smoked-salmon sandwiches he had sent in.

'You can use my private bathroom to freshen up,' he said when it was almost time for them to go. 'You've brought something along for tonight?'

Peta nodded, thinking uneasily about the dress that hung in a garment carrier on the back of her office door. She ought never to have let Sue persuade her to wear it. The black one would have been so much more suitable.

In the close intimacy of his car Peta felt his presence as if she never had before. She could feel every one of her nerve-ends skittering simply because she was sitting close to him, the skin on her bones tightening, and the most damning heat invading her body.

'What's wrong?'

My heart's thumping so loud it hurts, that's what's wrong, she thought. And it was complete and utter madness. She lifted her chin and dared to look at him. In profile, he was the essence of autocratic arrogance. A high forehead, a Roman nose, full lips, a firm chin. And, what she hadn't noticed before, long, thick eyelashes.

He turned to look at her. 'Well?'

'Nothing.'

'You're uptight about nothing?' he demanded crisply.

'Maybe because I don't think I'll live up to your expectations, Mr Papadakis.' Dammit, she hadn't meant to say that. She wanted him to think that she was Miss Efficiency. But something had made her say it; probably a need to point him away from the real reason that she was on edge.

'All you need to do is make notes. We talked about it earlier; I thought you understood. You haven't let me down so far. I have every faith in you.' Adding after a slight pause, 'I'd prefer it if you called me Andreas when we're alone.'

Peta only just stopped her mouth from falling open. Progress indeed! Not many people on the company, she was sure, called him Andreas. It was always Mr Papadakis, even from his most senior staff. His attitude didn't invite familiarity. 'Very well,' she agreed, but somehow she couldn't see herself doing it.

'That's good, Peta.'

She rather liked the way her name rolled off his tongue. He made it sound beautiful and exotic.

'So no more nerves, hey?' he asked as they pulled up on the hotel forecourt. And his smile did the most nerve-chilling things to her body. This wasn't the Andreas Papadakis she knew, and she didn't want him turning into anything else. She had grown used to his harshness. She could handle it. If he turned all soft on her she would end up a mushy mess.

But once the conference got under way she need not have worried. This was her employer at his most efficient. He was chairing the meeting, and every now and then when some pertinent point was made his eyes darted in her direction to make sure she had made a note of it. He need not have worried either. She was writing *everything* down.

Each delegate wore a name badge, so she knew exactly who was saying what, and she soon found herself either agreeing or disagreeing with the various statements. Once she almost jumped up to argue with a guy who said that the reason the shipping industry was going into decline was due to apathy on behalf of the ship owners.

It was Andreas himself who slapped him down. Peta found him fascinating to watch. In a dark grey cashmere suit, white silk shirt and a discreet red and grey tie, he was the epitome of a successful businessman. He was clearly respected and his points of view always carefully listened to. She saw several heads nod whenever he made a point; rarely did anyone disagree with him.

But she also saw Andreas the man, the incredibly sexy man. She was able to look at him without fear. She was able to look at those liquid brown eyes with their long curling lashes, at the sensuality of firm, full lips, and she even allowed herself to wonder what it would be like to be kissed by him.

With horror she realised that she had let her mind drift, that she hadn't heard what had just been said, and Andreas Papadakis's eyes were shooting daggers. The man never missed a thing! But thankfully he asked Peter Miller to repeat what he had said, as though he himself hadn't fully heard. And after that Peta was careful not to let her mind wander.

So much was said, so much discussed, that Peta knew it would take her hours to type up the notes. Hours she didn't have. Unless, of course, she could wangle a laptop out of him and take it home. It would solve the problem of asking Marnie to look after Ben and she would be able to spend precious hours with her son.

The afternoon fled and it was soon time for dinner; time to change into the dress that filled her with horror

whenever she thought about it. Andreas had booked her
a room and she was able to shower and take a short rest
before making up her face and doing her hair.

Peta rarely wore much make-up but this evening she
felt that she needed some protective armour, something
to make her feel good in the dark green dress. And so
on went the foundation and the blusher, the eye shadow
and mascara, and a much deeper-pink lipstick than she
normally used.

Finally she was ready, and at almost the same time
her employer tapped on the door. Peta awaited his reaction, dreading it, not surprised when he slowly and
carefully eyed her up and down. It sent a whole gamut
of emotions rushing through her as she stood there and
suffered his appraisal, notwithstanding the fact that he
looked totally devastating in his dinner suit.

He missed nothing. Not the way the satin material
defined the curve of her hips, the flatness of her stomach,
or the soft roundness of her breasts. It had been horren-
dously expensive, according to Sue, and made Peta look
taller and extremely elegant. And yet all she was aware
of was how low the neckline dipped and the way
Andreas Papadakis's eyes had lingered there.

She even caught a glimpse of desire, gone in an instant, and she might have imagined it because all he did
was slowly nod his head in approval. 'Let's join the
others,' he said crisply.

The more she thought about it the surer Peta was that
she'd been mistaken. He didn't even compliment her,
which was the least he could have done, considering the
way she'd put herself out for him.

Nevertheless she drew admiring glances from the
other delegates, which went some way to appeasing her,
and although conversation over the meal still rested on

business it was far less formal and there was no need
for her to take any notes.

She was extremely conscious of sitting by Andreas's
side and wished he had placed her somewhere else. She
was the only female present—obviously the other men
had seen no reason to bring their secretaries—and it was
only sheer stubbornness that made her get through the
evening without feeling uncomfortable.

Andreas, to give him his due, didn't ignore her. He
included her in all conversations, surprising her sometimes by asking her opinion, listening attentively when
she spoke. Peta had worked for the company long
enough to have formed her own ideas, and was able to
contribute successfully.

The only problem was sitting close to Andreas. He
had an indefinable charisma, which she was sure even
the men must feel, although not in the same way as she
did. He was capable of controlling a room full of people
with a word and a look, but she couldn't control the
tingle of her senses. It had begun faintly and grown with
every passing minute until her veins fairly sizzled.

It was idiotic of her to feel such a response, and yet
there was nothing she could do to stop it. She had never
for one moment expected, when she was summoned to
work for him, that he would evoke such feelings in her.
They were contrary to every thought she had, contrary
and undesirable. Sex had never played an important part
in her life, not after Joe, and she couldn't understand
why this man aroused her baser instincts now.

By the end of the evening she wished that she'd never
come, and when he offered to take her home Peta shook
her head. 'It's all right, I'll get a taxi.' In the confines
of his car her torture would be even worse.

'No, you won't,' he stated firmly, 'and if your refusal

is because I've had a few drinks, there's no need to worry because my driver is waiting for us.'

There was no way out.

Peta took her time collecting her coat and bag, willing her hormones to settle down and ignore this magnificently sexy male who just happened to be her boss. Lord, if only he knew! She'd be out of a job like a shot, or—an even more terrifying thought—he'd take advantage. He'd use her!

Her face was serious when she finally joined him in the hotel foyer. This last thought had scared her, made her realise how stupid she was being. 'I'm ready,' she said abruptly.

He gave her a strange look but said nothing, slipping into the car beside her and giving his driver her address. He sank back into the soft leather seat and closed his eyes. Peta huddled into her corner and closed her eyes, too, hoping to ignore him. Impossible! She could still smell his distinctive cologne, sense his powerful body so near to hers. There was enough space between them for another person but it made no difference. He was still far too close for comfort.

'You've done a good job today, Peta.'

His voice made her eyes snap open. He was looking at her from beneath half-closed lids. A lazy, sensual look that set her nerves on edge again.

'I appreciate it. And good work needs rewarding.' He leaned towards her and Peta panicked. What sort of reward was he talking about? A kiss? More than that? She shrank even further into the seat.

'You'll see a handsome bonus in your pay cheque at the end of the month.'

Peta breathed a sigh of relief. 'I've not typed my notes out yet,' she pointed out. 'You might be disappointed.'

'I don't think so. You're by far the best assistant I've had in a long time.'

'In that case,' she said, taking advantage of one of his rare moments of companionship, 'could I take a laptop home to do the notes? I really won't have time at the office and I don't want to work late and leave Ben again.'

'Consider it done,' he said. 'He needs you as much as I do.'

Peta must have shown her surprise because he added, 'Believe me, Peta, I do appreciate that you have a home life. I press people hard, I know—it's the only way to get anything done—but I too have a life outside work.'

'You do? I thought there was nothing more important than turning around ailing businesses.'

'I know I give that impression. I've always worked hard.'

'So what do you do outside work hours?' she asked, amazing herself by her temerity.

'I too have a son,' he admitted. 'A son who complains that he never sees enough of me.'

His confession stunned Peta. Of all the rumours that had spread through the company, this wasn't one of them.

'You look surprised.'

'I am. I didn't know; I didn't realise; I thought...' Her voice tailed off in confusion.

'You thought I was a workaholic, maybe even a bit of a playboy in my spare time? I do know what's being said about me, Peta.'

'But you don't care to correct it?'

'My private life is just that—private. I prefer it to remain that way.'

'You can rest assured I'll say nothing,' she said, and at that moment they drew up outside her house.

'Wait!' He leaned forward and put a hand over hers when she made to open the door. 'Gareth will let you out.'

His touch meant nothing and yet it took her breath away. She turned her head to look at him and his brown eyes darkened and his lips brushed her cheek. Just that, nothing more, yet it felt as though he was making love to her.

'Thank you, Peta, for brightening up my evening. You look truly beautiful.'

Peta was saved answering by his driver opening her door. She climbed out speedily, turning only at the last minute to smile weakly at her boss. The compliment was late, yet it made more of an impact because of it. Her fingers trembled as she put the key in the lock, and the car didn't move until she had safely closed the door behind her.

CHAPTER THREE

ANDREAS pondered his problem. He could, of course, get another girl from the agency, but how many was that now? And Nikos had liked none of them. There had to be another answer. He drank cup after cup of black coffee until finally a solution came to him. It put a smile on his face as he showered and got ready for work, and he was impatient for Peta to arrive.

When she did he called her straight into his office. Andreas Papadakis didn't believe in beating around the bush. If he had something to say he came straight out with it. In his opinion it was the only way.

'Miss James…Peta, I need your help.'

He saw the way she frowned, pulling her delicately shaped brows together. He saw the way she bit her lower lip, which she always did when she wasn't sure what to expect of him. Gone was the sexy dress of last night, replaced by one of her smart suits. The dress had amazed him. He had never imagined her wearing anything so revealing. Amazed and pleased him. He'd heard a few whispered comments about what a lucky so-and-so he was to have an assistant like that. And it had certainly made him look at her in a new light.

Not that he hadn't already realised her potential. She was an exceedingly attractive girl who never made the most of her assets. That gorgeous auburn hair, for instance, was always tied uncompromisingly back, and those lovely dark blue eyes were never shown off to their advantage. Last night, when she'd carefully made them up, he had felt their full impact for the first time. The things they'd done to him were best forgotten. She was such an ice-cold maiden that if she'd read the ignoble thoughts in his mind she would have very likely walked out of her job. And now he needed her more than ever.

'Can you think of anyone in the secretarial pool who'd do your job as well as you?'

'You're sacking me?' The colour faded from her cheeks, her eyes widening in dismay.

'Of course not,' he assured her quickly. 'I have something else in mind.'

Her chin lifted in another of her delightful habits and she looked at him warily.

'I need someone to look after Nikos.'

'Your son?'

'Yes.'

'And you're asking me. Why?'

'Because his current nanny's handed in her notice.'

Her incredibly blue eyes flashed her indignance and he wondered why the hell he hadn't noticed long before now how gorgeous they were. They were enough to send any man crazy.

'I'm a qualified secretary, not a child-minder,' she retorted. 'I don't want to spend my life looking after someone else's children.'

Andreas hadn't expected her to say yes straight away, he had known she would need a lot of persuading, but she sounded so adamant that he feared she would never agree. Perhaps he ought to give her no choice, either she take the job or... No, if he did that he'd risk losing out both ways. 'You hate having to leave Ben every day, don't you?' he asked quietly.

She nodded. 'More than you'll ever know.'

'Oh, I do; you underestimate me. This is the perfect

solution. It will solve your dilemma as well as mine. You and Ben would move into my house, you'd be there for him whenever he needed you, and you could also do some work for me from home.' To him it was the simplest solution, the obvious one.

The look on her face spoke a thousand words. 'Mr Papadakis, living with you is the last thing I want. Ben and I are happy as we are. I love my little house. Why should I give it up? And, for that matter, where's your wife? Why can't she bring up her own child?'

Andreas's eyes shadowed as his thoughts raced back to the blackest days of his life. 'My wife's dead,' he told her bluntly, 'and you wouldn't need to give up your house; you could let it.' He saw the uncertainty in her eyes and pressed home his faint advantage. 'Sit down. Think again about the benefits.'

Reluctantly she perched herself on the edge of a chair, crossing her legs so that her skirt rode up. Not for the first time he felt a stirring in his loins. But that sort of thing had to be put to one side. He needed her to feel safe, not threatened. He hadn't failed to notice in the car last night how she had drawn back from him when he kissed her cheek. Someone, somewhere along the line, had destroyed her trust in men, and he had no intention of adding to it.

'I desperately need someone to look after Nikos. You know how much time I put in here—the poor little guy hardly sees me.'

'So why don't *you* work from home?'

It was a logical question and he grimaced. 'I'd love to, but if I'm to turn this company around I need to keep my finger on the pulse.'

'How long would you expect me to do the job?'

'I don't know. Until I find someone else, perhaps,

maybe even indefinitely if it works as well as I hope it will. You won't lose out, I assure you.'

'What if Nikos doesn't like me?'

'He will.' How could he not? Peta James was good with children, he'd seen that for himself. She was also exciting and provocative. He'd noticed at the conference how easily she talked to other people. In fact she had seemed far more at ease with some of them than with him. He hadn't liked it. He'd fancied her that night more than he'd ever expected.

'In fact,' he went on, 'it might be a good idea to take you to see him before we finally sign the deal.'

'Sign the deal?' she repeated with a frown.

'Figuratively speaking, of course,' he said with what he hoped was a reassuring smile. Smiling didn't come easy to him these days. There were too many pressures, too much to do, too many sad memories, and Nikos was the one who suffered. If he could persuade Peta to take this job it would be the best thing that had happened to his son in a long time. It might not be so good for him, here, because she was incredibly efficient, but his son's well-being meant more to him than anything else.

'We'll finish work early tonight and I'll take you to meet him,' he said decisively.

'I can't,' Peta said with the now familiar toss of her head. 'Ben's playing football. I try never to miss a match.'

It was Andreas's turn to frown. 'Bronwen leaves at the end of the week. I need to have everything sorted well before then. How about after the football match? Bring Ben with you. It will be good for the boys to meet.'

'How old is Nikos?' she asked, and he could see her mind turning over the situation.

'Seven,' he answered, 'though he's very grown-up for his age.'

'Does he have a Scalextric?'

'You bet.'

'Then I'm sure Ben will get on with him,' she said with a faint smile.

And the way she said it reassured him that her answer would ultimately be yes.

Peta's mind was in a whirl. Her first instinct had been to turn Andreas down. She still might, because would it be wise, feeling as she did about him? It was scary the way he'd managed to set her feelings alight last night. Scary and undesirable. She'd been hurt too much in the past to want to get involved. It was far better to keep things on a purely professional level. But would she be able to do that living in the same house?

She placed the last lot of post on his desk for signing. 'How do I get to your house?' She had no idea where he lived. Again the rumour machine had him living in a fantastic mansion overlooking Southampton Water with a whole host of servants at his beck and call.

'No need to drive; I'll pick you up. What time does the match finish?'

About to say he didn't have to put himself out, Peta decided against it. She was the one doing the favour so why should she do the running?

Peta clapped and yelled enthusiastically every time Ben's team scored a goal. And when Ben himself scored she went wild with delight. 'Well done, Ben!' she shouted, jumping up and down, clapping her hands. 'Go for it!'

Another much louder voice echoed her words from behind. 'Well done, Ben!'

She turned and there was an instant's sizzling reaction as she met the eyes of Andreas Papadakis. She was the first to look away, praying fervently that he wasn't able to read her mind. It was all so wrong, this physical attraction. Despite her telling her body to behave itself, it had gone into involuntary spasm and there was nothing she could do about it.

At his side was a boy roughly Ben's height, dark-haired and dark-eyed, but with a much rounder face than his father's and a thinner mouth. 'How did you find us?' she asked. They'd arranged for him to pick her up at her house, which was a five-minute walk away.

'I followed the noise. It sounds an exciting match.'

'It is,' she agreed. 'And this is Nikos, I take it?'

'It is, indeed. Nikos, this is the lady I told you about, the one who's going to look after you when Bronwen leaves.'

Nikos looked up at her with serious brown eyes. 'I don't like Bronwen. She shouts a lot.'

Peta wondered whether he deserved it, whether he played her up when his father was absent. 'Ben's dying to meet you,' she said with a warm smile.

When she'd told Ben they might be moving he'd been at first upset and then excited, especially when he learned that there'd be someone his own age to play with, and they'd probably be living in a much bigger house.

'It will be good to have some company,' said Nikos. 'I get bored on my own. Which one is Ben? I like football. I'd like to play with them.'

Peta's eyes met Andreas's and she smiled, remembering him telling her how grown-up Nikos was for his age. And she was amazed at how good his English was, too. Ben hadn't even started to learn a foreign language yet.

'Doesn't your school have a football team?'

'Yes, but I am never allowed to take part. Dad is always too busy, and none of my nannies has liked football.'

Again Peta looked at Andreas. His lips turned down at the corners and he shook his head, suggesting that he knew nothing about it. Which was about par for the course, she decided. Andreas spent far too much time working, relying heavily on other people to look after his son. It was no wonder he didn't know the thoughts that went through Nikos's head.

'Well, I like it,' she said. 'So go ahead and join your team; I'll always come and cheer you on.'

'You will?' His eyes shone with delight. 'Thank you. Thank you very much. Did you hear that, Dad? I think I am going to like my new nanny.'

Peta only hoped that his matches wouldn't clash with Ben's. She would hate to let Nikos down now that she'd made her promise.

When the match was over Peta wanted to take Ben home to shower and change, but Andreas insisted that it didn't matter, and in the back of the car the two boys soon got to know one another.

'They're getting on well,' murmured Andreas.

Peta nodded. 'Ben's a good mixer. What made you come so early?'

He gave a guilty grimace. 'When I explained to Nikos where we were going it was his idea. I hadn't realised he was so interested in football.'

'Most small boys are.'

'Am I being chastised?'

She looked at him then, and it was a big mistake.

There was a hint of wry humour on his face, something she had never seen before. He was no longer the Tyrant but a father, with a son he loved but didn't know much about. And he was sharing that knowledge with her.

It felt oddly like a bond, and she could so easily fall into the trap of revealing her feelings. But that wasn't what he wanted, and neither did she, for that matter. Andreas needed someone to care for his son when he was unable to. And he had placed that trust in her. She dared not let him down by showing a marked preference for his body.

For once the rumour machine was right. He did live in a big house, though it wasn't overlooking Southampton Water. It was set in its own grounds, hidden from the road, suddenly emerging as they rounded a bend in the drive. It was a red-brick and timber building, several hundred years old, by the look of it, with ivy clambering over some of the walls, tall chimneys reaching for the sky, every window gleaming in the late-evening sun.

'I don't own, I rent,' he told her, seeing the look of awe and amazement on her face. 'I took it while I looked around for somewhere suitable, but to tell you the truth I haven't had time, and actually I like it here. I'm considering making the owner an offer.'

Nikos and Ben were already out of the car and running towards the house. Andreas and Peta followed. She felt uncomfortable walking beside him; it felt wrong to be going to her employer's house, to even consider living with him. She wasn't a nanny; how could he expect her to do a nanny's job? Her only qualification was bringing up her own son. The tempting part was that she would see more of Ben. No more leaving him with Marnie while she worked late, or even when he came home from school. She would be there for him always. The thought brought a smile to her lips.

Andreas wasn't looking at her, and yet he must have sensed her smiling because he turned and spoke. 'You're happy about the situation?'

'I guess so. I was thinking about being able to spend more time with Ben.' What she didn't dare think about was spending time with Andreas. Not that she expected to see very much of him. With her safely ensconced in his house looking after his precious son, he would be able to stay at the office for as long as he liked.

And if he brought work home for her to do that would be even better, because there would be hours in the day while the boys were at school when she would have nothing to do. Unless he expected her to look after the house as well? She didn't mind cooking for Nikos but what else would he expect of her? Exactly what were a nanny's duties?

The boys had raced upstairs, where, presumably, Nikos had his Scalextric laid out. Peta stood in the entrance hall and looked around her. Impressive wasn't the word. A carved oak staircase curved its way up to a galleried landing. Stained-glass windows cast coloured reflections, and oil paintings, presumably of owners past, decorated the walls. It was like something she'd seen in a film but never first-hand.

He led the way along a lengthy corridor to a huge, comfortable kitchen, where a buxom middle-aged woman stood making pastry. 'I wasn't expecting you yet, Mr Papadakis,' she said, looking flustered. 'Nor was Bronwen. She's gone out to meet her boyfriend.'

A harsh frown creased his brow. 'Perhaps it's as well she's leaving,' he said tersely. 'Bess, I'd like you to meet

Bronwen's replacement, Peta James. Peta, this is Bess Middleton, my housekeeper.'

The woman's thin brows rose into untidy grey hair. I wonder how long you'll last? she seemed to be saying.

'Hello, Bess.' Peta held out her hand, then laughed when she realised the other woman's was covered in flour. 'I'm not starting until next week. Andreas thought I ought to have a look over the place.'

'You've met Nikos, I take it?' the woman asked.

Peta nodded. 'I have a son about Nikos's age. They'll be good company for each other. They're upstairs now.'

'I see. Good luck, then. I hope you'll last longer than the others.'

Peta looked at Andreas. She hadn't realised he was watching her and her face flushed at his intense scrutiny. It was faintly disapproving. Was it because she'd called him Andreas in front of his housekeeper?

'Come,' he said abruptly, 'I'll show you the rest of the house.' It was a whistle-stop tour and entirely unnecessary in her opinion, because she'd need a map to find her way around. On the ground floor there were five different reception rooms and a study, while upstairs there were six bedrooms, each with an *ensuite* bathroom, as well as a spacious room in the attic. It was here that they found Nikos and Ben happily playing with the Scalextric. There was so much of it that it must have cost a small fortune.

'Mummy,' said Ben excitedly, 'look at all this.'

'It's wonderful, darling, but I think we ought to be going.'

'No!' came the disgruntled response. 'Not yet—we've only just got here.'

'And you're going to live here soon,' she reminded him, 'so come on, you'll have plenty of time to play.'

Andreas had hardly spoken on their tour. He'd pointed out which would be her room and which one Ben's, and she'd seen his bedroom, in shades of burgundy and dark green—an entirely impersonal room with not even a pair of slippers on view. He probably didn't have time to wear slippers, she'd thought bitterly. He was too manic about work.

'Leave them,' he said now. 'We'll go to my study and discuss your duties.'

'Very well.' She kept her tone crisp and her eyes directly on his, and as soon as they were seated in the oak-panelled room she asked, 'What have I said that's made you angry?'

He shook his head. 'I'm not annoyed with you; it's Bronwen. She had no idea that I wouldn't need her tonight. She might be working her notice but she has no right to take liberties. I've half a mind to tell her to go now.'

'Except that I can't start straight away,' declared Peta. 'There's too much to sort out.'

'Like what?' he demanded.

'I have to pack, for one thing. Finalise bills, see about letting, tell everyone where I've gone, especially my parents…a hundred and one things.' Her parents lived in Cornwall, where she herself had been brought up. She'd stayed in Southampton after finishing university, and now only went home on the occasional weekend and during holiday periods. But her mother rang often, wanting to know how she was coping, how Ben was, and why didn't she come home to live? What would she say when she heard that her precious daughter was moving in with the boss?

'I can organise most things for you,' he informed.

'I'm sure you can, but I'd prefer to do it myself,' she

said tightly. 'You can see to the letting, if you wish, but everything else I'll do.'

'One of the new era of independent females.' He leaned back in his leather chair and studied her. 'I'm not sure whether I like it. I think I prefer the chivalrous days when a woman depended on a man, when he cosseted and protected her, when he made her feel feminine and beautiful and very, very much wanted.'

His eyes smouldered, his voice growled, and he looked at her with far more intent than he ever had before. Peta felt her nerve ends quiver. Was he trying to tell her something or was it her imagination? Was she reading what she wanted to read? Or was he interested? Would it be wise to move in with him? Had he manufactured this job especially so that he could get her into his bed?

'Now what are you thinking?'

'Why?'

'You look as though you believe I have designs on you.'

Oh, Lord, was she that transparent? Peta felt her cheeks flame. 'You couldn't be further from the truth,' she said distantly.

'You have a very expressive face, Peta. Didn't you know?'

'And you are jumping to entirely the wrong conclusions. I'm not interested in any man, Mr Papadakis.'

'Andreas.'

She grimaced. 'Very well, Andreas, although I don't think it's a good idea. Did you see the way your housekeeper looked at me when I called you Andreas?'

'She was probably wondering how you'd managed to get past the formality stage. Not many people do, I assure you. I find it doesn't pay.'

Peta wasn't sure she agreed with that. The senior staff at Linam Shipping would almost certainly feel much happier if they were on first-name terms with him. 'So I'm honoured?' she asked.

A faint smile quirked the corners of his mouth. 'You could say that.'

'Why?'

He thought for a long moment. 'Let's say I felt it would improve our relationship.'

'You mean you thought you'd get more work out of me?' she asked smartly, but she couldn't stop a faint smile.

'I don't always think about work, Peta. Ninety-nine per cent of the time, perhaps, but I do have red blood in my veins. I'm not entirely without feelings.'

Peta gave an inward groan. Was she jumping into a situation she would quickly regret? Ought she to tell him to stuff his job? Except that she would be upsetting both boys if she did. Ben would never forgive her; he was so looking forward to living here and having a friend to play with. To say nothing of the extra time she'd be able to spend with him. It was by far the best thing that had happened to her.

'So,' she said, pushing these thoughts to the back of her mind, 'tell me exactly what my duties are going to be.'

It was arranged that she take Nikos to and from school, plan his meals, cook them if Bess wasn't there, supervise his homework and make sure he always had a supply of clean clothes. All housework would be done by Bess Middleton and a local girl who came in twice a week.

'Is there anything else you want to ask me?'

Peta shook her head. 'Nothing that I can think of at the moment.'

'So it's settled. You'll start on Sunday?'

'I'll move in late on Sunday,' she corrected. 'I'll need the weekend to tie everything up.'

He nodded, looking well-pleased, and when they stood he shook her hand. 'Thank you, Peta. I do appreciate all that you're giving up.'

The scorching heat that ran through her at his touch told her that she was giving up far more than a little cottage and a certain lifestyle. She was in grave danger of giving up her freedom.

CHAPTER FOUR

As PETA locked the door and walked to her car, where Ben was already wriggling excitedly on his seat, she wondered for the thousandth time whether she was doing the right thing. She'd thought about it a lot since she'd given her word, and several times had considered backing out. The one thing that had stopped her was the thought that she'd see more of her precious son.

She really had hated having to go out to work, leaving Marnie to pick him up from school. She'd missed seeing the excitement on his face when he told the older woman all that he'd been doing. Obviously he'd told her, too, when she got home, but the initial enthusiasm had gone. And especially in school holidays—there had been so much she could be doing with him, so many places they could have gone. Instead she'd had to rely on her neighbour to keep him entertained while she earned the money to clothe and feed them and run her house.

There was also Nikos to consider. She couldn't get out of her mind his cheerful face when she'd mentioned watching him play football. She could imagine how her own son would feel if she never went to see him play. To Ben, having his mother watch and encourage him was the most important thing in the world. It was a pity Andreas didn't see things that way. Poor Nikos was missing out on such a lot—and so too was Andreas, if only he knew it.

When they arrived Andreas was outside waiting for them.

Smiling.

The smile stunned her. It was unlike any other smile he had given her. It was a predatory smile. It heated her blood and sent a violent reaction through her body. This was definitely a big mistake. She hadn't agreed to do the job because she'd thought the move would be good for Ben, or because it would help Nikos, but because of this man. This lean, sensual man with the devastating good looks and compelling dark eyes. It was a disturbing discovery.

And it was suddenly clear that he was equally hungry for her! She was now his victim. And yet, even as she stared at him in chilling horror, the smile changed. It became a warmly welcoming one, a friendly one, nothing in it to suggest that he had designs on her. Had she imagined it? Was she becoming neurotic because of her own unstoppable, unwanted emotions?

'I was beginning to think you'd changed your mind.' He came hurriedly down the steps as she climbed out of the car, damningly attractive in an open-necked shirt that revealed a scattering of dark curly hairs on his hard-muscled chest. 'Let me help you unload.'

'Where's Nikos?' asked Ben eagerly as he too scrambled out.

'Already in bed,' Andreas answered. 'He tried to wait up but sleep got the better of him.'

'I'm not tired,' said Ben bravely, at the same time fighting back a yawn.

'In that case you can carry some stuff up to your room,' snapped Peta when she saw that he was going to dash indoors empty-handed.

Her tone was sharper than she'd intended and she saw Andreas frown. She oughtn't to have rounded on her son; it wasn't Ben she was annoyed with—it was herself for imagining something that wasn't there. Andreas couldn't care less about her; he was interested only in Nikos's well-being. That was what she was here for, nothing else, and she'd do well to remember it.

Once all the stuff was piled into their rooms he offered Mrs Middleton's help to unpack but Peta declined. 'I can manage,' she said tensely.

'As you wish,' he agreed with a laconic shrug. 'When you've put Ben to bed come and join me. I'll be in my study.'

There was a lot to unpack and it took her ages; Ben was asleep before she'd finished, but even then she was reluctant to go downstairs.

She remembered the room, quite a big room, oak-panelled with an immense desk across one corner. In front of the window, with excellent views of the land-scaped gardens, were two easy chairs, and it was in one of these that she found him.

He'd left his door wide for her to walk in, though she tapped on it first to alert him to her presence. 'Welcome to your new home,' he said to her now. 'I think this calls for a celebratory drink. What would you like?'

Peta didn't much care for alcohol; it held too many bad memories. She'd had wine on the day of the con-ference, but only because she hadn't wanted to cause a fuss, and even then she'd taken only a few sips. 'A soft drink, I think. Coke or lemonade, I don't mind which.'

She sat down on the chair next to him, stifling the tingle of electricity that alerted her senses to the very real danger he posed.

'Are you sure that's all you want?'

Peta nodded and turned her head to watch Andreas as he walked to a cunningly concealed bar and flipped the top off a bottle before pouring Coke into a glass.

'I really do appreciate what you're doing for me,' he said when he returned to his seat, handing the drink to her.

Their fingers touched and Peta jumped, some of the Coke going down her clean white skirt. She swore beneath her breath.

'How clumsy of me,' said Andreas swiftly.

'It wasn't your fault,' she assured him, conscious of the sudden heat in her cheeks. 'I'd best go and change; rinse it out before it stains.'

'You *are* coming back?' he asked, and for the first time Peta noticed lines of strain on his face. He was probably apprehensive about how things would work out with her and Nikos, and all the problems at work wouldn't help either, and here she was worrying over her own stupid reactions.

'Of course,' she agreed with a faint smile, even though she'd actually planned on staying upstairs, where it was safer. At the office she could ignore his sexuality and concentrate on the work in hand. Here it was a different story. The trouble was, if she didn't go back down he'd more than likely come charging up to see where she was.

She had not realised when she'd agreed to take the job as Nikos's nanny that she would spend any time with Andreas. It was too intimate, too disturbing, too everything. The blood fairly sizzled through her veins, and the thought of them sitting close together watching the sky darken as the sun went down was enough to send her frantic with fear.

Peta deliberately took her time rinsing the skirt, and when she finally plucked up the courage to rejoin Andreas it was to find him fast asleep in his chair, legs outstretched, his head resting on a cushion. The perfect excuse to creep upstairs, she thought, but somehow her legs wouldn't carry her away. She stood there looking at him, drinking in the beautiful, sculpted lines of his face, the way his hair curled crisply around his ears, the fullness of his lips, curved upwards at the corners as though he was having a pleasant dream.

It wasn't long before her eyes wandered down to the rise and fall of his chest. The dark hairs, some of which she could see at the V of his shirt, were visible through the fine silk. Her fingers itched to touch. He had a tremendous body, finely honed, with not an ounce of superfluous fat anywhere.

His narrow hips next, and the hard flatness of his stomach. She quickly skimmed over the next bit, feeling a tightening of her stomach muscles as she did so, before considering the long length of his powerful legs. He really was a tremendously exciting male animal. The first man in a long, long time who had aroused any feelings in her.

Suddenly, without warning, his hand shot out and caught her wrist, pulling her down onto his lap. 'Like what you see, do you?' he growled in her ear.

Peta's cheeks flamed as she felt the hardness of his arousal. Thank goodness he couldn't tell what was going on inside her own body. 'What the hell do you think you're doing?' she demanded, struggling to free herself. 'If this is the reason you've got me here then—'

Her words were cut off by an angry snarl. 'Pardon me, lady, you were the one doing the looking, and judging by your expression you were highly interested—and, if my judgement isn't wrong, highly aroused as well.'

Peta's eyes blazed. 'Pardon me also, but you couldn't be further from the truth. If you want to know what I was thinking, it was how I'd managed to allow myself to be sucked into this arrangement. If I'd wanted to be a nanny I'd have trained as one.' And with that she managed to wrench free.

He laughed. A deep belly laugh that didn't amuse her.

'I'm glad you find it funny; I don't,' she said caustically and loudly.

'It's your indignation I find amusing,' he said, proceeding to push himself up. 'You really were caught in the act. But never mind, consider it forgotten. I value you too much to spend time arguing.'

How could she forget such an embarrassing moment? Especially as he'd read her thoughts and feelings so accurately—it didn't bear thinking about.

Not until Peta had gone to her room did Andreas allow himself to mull over that telling moment. It wasn't the first time he'd been eyed up so thoroughly, and it probably wouldn't be the last. He was a reluctant target for sex-hungry females. But he hadn't expected it of Peta James.

She'd always given the impression of being completely uninterested in him. In any man, for that matter. She lived for her son alone. Everything she did was for Ben. He admired her for her devotion. Meanwhile he had discovered another dimension in her make-up. An interesting one.

And one day he might do something about it. But not yet. He didn't want to frighten her away before she'd even begun the job, even though his own hormones were having a field-day and he felt a shocking need to take her to bed. He wanted to lose himself in her body; he wanted to touch, to taste, to get to know intimately every single inch of her.

She was an exciting woman, was Peta James, a

woman of many layers. At work she was the perfect PA. The most efficient he'd ever had. More often than not she anticipated his needs. He was going to miss her a great deal in that respect.

Then there was Peta the siren. That was how she had looked in that green satin dress. And yet still she had retained her cool demeanour. She'd seemed not to notice the admiring glances certainly hadn't played on it, but he'd have liked to bet that there wasn't a man in the room who hadn't fancied her. As he had himself.

And now, a few minutes ago, she was a hot-blooded woman ripe for making love. He had seen the depth of hunger in her eyes when she'd thought him asleep. How long since Ben's father had disappeared out of her life? How long since she'd had a man?

Her house was small but carefully and thoughtfully furnished. It was a home, not just a house. She had lovingly made it into a comfortable home. Not the way Maria had, or his mother—both of their houses had been showplaces. Peta's was so comfortable, so lived-in, that he'd felt completely relaxed there.

And he had taken her away from it!

The thought was not a pleasant one. And yet if she hadn't agreed to come he'd have probably threatened to sack her. He'd been prepared to go to any lengths to get what he wanted. A deep frown gouged his brow. Was that really the type of guy he was? He'd had to be ruthless to get where he was, but to put someone out of a job when they had a child to clothe and feed and a house to run wasn't quite playing the game. He'd done it in the past, though, without a second thought. He put his fingers to his temples and rubbed at the nagging pain. What was this woman doing to him?

*   *   *

Peta woke from a troubled sleep. She'd been dreaming but she couldn't remember what the dream was about, only that it had left her feeling deeply disturbed. And when she opened her eyes she thought that she must still be asleep, because this wasn't her room. This was a spacious bedroom decorated in cool greens and cream. Hers was tiny and cosy in pink and lavender.

It was a few seconds before the reality of the situation hit her and her first thoughts were of Ben. How would he feel, waking in a strange room? Last night he'd been too tired even to notice his surroundings, but this morning he might be afraid.

She leapt out of bed and without even bothering to pull on her dressing gown dashed out of her room—and catapulted straight into Andreas Papadakis.

His strong arms steadied her. 'Whoa, there; what's the rush?' he asked in amusement.

'I must go to Ben.' Her voice came out strange and breathless. The heat of his body flamed her senses. She felt as though she was spinning out of control. It was an instant thing, one she could do without and one she needed to fight. 'He might be frightened waking up in a strange place.'

Andreas smiled calmly, but it did nothing to steady her racing pulses. His hands still held her, his hard body grazing her own through the thin material of her night-dress, and his velvet-brown eyes looked down into hers.

He was enjoying it, she realised. Enjoying making her feel uncomfortable.

'Ben and Nikos are having breakfast,' he informed. 'Bess is looking after them.'

'What time is it?' she demanded, finally wrestling herself free, conscious now that with space between them he could look at the way her breasts had peaked against the soft cotton.

'Just turned eight.'

'What?' She was horrified. She was always up by seven on days she had to go to work. 'He'll be late for school. I'll be late for work. And you're usually at the office by this time.' He hadn't shaved yet, she noticed; he must have risen late as well. She liked the dark stubble on his strong square jaw. It made him less severe, more of an action man than a dark-suited tycoon.

'I think you're forgetting, Peta, that your job now is here. There's plenty of time for you to get Ben to school. I'll take Nikos today; I want a word with his teacher.'

She had forgotten. In the panic of waking up in a strange place she'd completely lost it. She was no longer his PA but Nikos's nanny. And she'd already failed in her breakfast duty. Not that Andreas seemed to mind, which was a surprise. He was a different man here. More dangerous. More threatening to her sanity. And her body!

With a tiny cry of distress she swung away and returned to her bedroom.

The day went surprisingly quickly. Karen, her replacement, phoned a couple of times with queries about work, and Andreas himself phoned her once. Other than that she spent the day typing up notes from the conference. At Andreas's suggestion she set herself up in his study, using the laptop that he had put at her disposal. It wasn't an ideal arrangement as far as Peta was concerned because it was too easy to imagine him there. The room was eternally filled with his presence and the lingering smell of his cologne, so much so that she began to doubt her sanity in agreeing to his suggestion.

It was a relief when she left the house to pick up Nikos from his private school and then Ben from Marnie's. Marnie had been sad to see her leave, but delighted that she still had the privilege of meeting Ben out of school and taking him to her house, if only for a short time, to await his mother's arrival.

In the car on the way home the two boys chatted incessantly, making Peta realise how lonely Ben had been before. She'd always envisaged having two or three children quite close together—until fate had decreed otherwise.

Andreas didn't get home until after the boys were in bed and Peta had already eaten. She was passing through the hall when he arrived. He was still in work mode; she could tell by the distant look in his eyes, the intense frown on his forehead. How had his day gone without her? she wondered. How had he got on with Karen? And how had Karen coped with his often unrealistic demands?

But it was not something she dared to ask. Theirs wasn't the sort of relationship where they could sit and discuss the day's events. She was still his employee. She had her own sitting room, and it was to this that she took herself now.

She flicked through the channels on the TV, but found nothing much there, so she curled into a corner of the sofa with a book. It was number one in the best-seller lists and she was lost in a world of espionage and double-dealing when Andreas came to find her.

At first she didn't see him; it was not until he cleared his throat that she looked up and realised that he was standing watching her.

'Must be a good book.'

'It is.' He had showered and shaved and changed into

navy cotton trousers and a pale blue shirt. The worry lines had gone and in his hand was a tot of whisky. She felt her insides sear and shrivel as those chestnut eyes penetrated hers. Not with intent—there was nothing in his expression to suggest that he fancied her—but it was as though he was trying to look deep into her soul. To find out what made her tick, what her innermost secrets were.

She straightened her legs and put down the book.

'Won't you join me?' he asked, raising his glass.

Peta shook her head. 'I don't drink.'

'Not ever?'

'Maybe occasionally,' she said with a shrug. 'A toast for a wedding, something like that, but in the main, no.'

'Why's that? I don't think I've ever met anyone who doesn't drink. May I?' He indicated the chair opposite.

Peta couldn't really say no when it was his own house, even if he had given her this room for her own private use, so she nodded, at the same time drawing in a deeply troubled breath. Her past history wasn't something she wanted to share. It wasn't something she was proud of. But at some time or another he would insist on knowing, so perhaps now was as good a time as any.

'I used to,' she confessed. 'Like the rest of my student friends I used to hang around in pubs, but one day I had too much. So much that I didn't know what I was doing.' She paused as memories of that night vividly reclaimed her mind. 'Ben is the result. I'm deeply ashamed of it, but I wouldn't be without him for the world.' She stuck her chin in the air as she spoke, challenging him to say something derogatory.

But he didn't. He looked at her thoughtfully instead. 'So what happened to Ben's father? Does he know about him?'

Peta nodded. 'He was my boyfriend at the time, my first love. We were inseparable. I thought I would spend the rest of my life with him. But as soon as I told him I was pregnant he didn't want to know me. In fact he refused to believe the baby was his.'

She clamped her lips. Joe had totally destroyed her trust in men. He'd even started going out with her best friend immediately afterwards, proving that he'd never really loved her, not the way she had loved him. And in the dark weeks that had followed she'd heard dozens of similar tales from sympathetic student friends, convincing her that she'd be far better off without a man in her life.

'So you've not seen him since?'

'No. Nor do I want to.'

'Don't you think that one day your son might want to know exactly who his father is?'

It was a logical question, one she had asked herself many times. 'I'll cross that bridge when I come to it,' she declared, and, with a desperate need to change the subject, 'I've finished the conference notes. They're on your desk.'

'Good girl. I could have done with you at the office today. Karen's a quick typist but she goes to pieces in an emergency.'

All of his requests were emergencies, remembered Peta. 'It could be that you make her nervous,' she said with great daring, remembering how she had felt that first day.

Dark brows rode smoothly upwards. 'If the girl can't do the job, then—'

'She gets her marching orders,' finished Peta crisply. 'You think that solves everything, don't you?'

To her amazement he smiled, a warm lazy smile that

sent her pulses into spasm. 'Do you know, Peta, no other woman has ever tried to put me in my place?'

'I hardly think I've done that,' she said, taking a deep breath to try and regulate the uneven beating of her heart. That smile had done things to her which she'd rather not happen. 'But I do believe in sticking up for myself. In my opinion, most men in official capacities think they can walk all over any woman who works for them. Lord knows why. It has to be an inbred thing.'

She watched the way his nostrils flared as she spoke and wondered whether she had gone too far, but then the white smile flashed again. 'You're probably right. Should I give her another chance?'

'I think you should give her at least a month's trial.'

'A month?' he queried sharply. 'You were fully efficient in less than a week.'

'I had a strong motive,' she said.

He frowned.

'Ben. I couldn't afford to be thrown out on my ear. I had to learn quickly.'

'And was I a hard taskmaster?' He leaned back comfortably in his chair, legs outstretched, looking as though he was in for a long stay.

'The worst,' she admitted. 'But the more difficult you were the more determined I was to stay the course.'

He suddenly leaned forward, elbows on his knees. 'You're some girl, Peta James.'

Her eyes were drawn to his and she could feel herself beginning to drown in their sensual, velvety depths. Her heart rate increased, her skin overheated, and without her realising it she inched closer to him. Any second now he was going to kiss her. She could sense it; was ready for it. The tip of her tongue moistened dry lips and her breathing grew shallow.

Then with a swift change of expression he rocked back in his seat. 'I had a kidnap threat today,' he said tensely. 'My son's life is in danger.'

Andreas was still reeling. The tersely worded note had shocked and horrified him, sent his senses spiralling endlessly in space. It had jolted him into the realisation of how very much Nikos meant to him. He had been too busy working to... No, he wouldn't go down that path. His son was his entire universe. Without him life would have no meaning.

Be warned, the note had said, *I'm going to kidnap your son. You will never see him again unless you pay me one million pounds.*

It took Andreas's mind back to another place, another time, when his younger brother, Christos, had been kidnapped and his own parents had nearly gone out of their minds with worry. After Nikos was born he had harboured the vague fear that the same thing might happen, but never really believed that it would. Until now...

Peta's eyes were wide as she looked at him, her own shock mirrored in their amethyst depths. 'Have you been to the police?'

His lips twisted in bitter irony. 'They politely suggested it's a practical joke. They said that if someone was going to kidnap Nikos they wouldn't give me any warning; they'd simply snatch him.'

'But you don't believe them?'

'Would you, if it were Ben?'

'I'd be scared to let him out of my sight,' she agreed, looking as worried as he felt. 'Do you know who's making the threat? And why?'

He silently thanked her for her concern. He needed someone at a time like this. 'Money, of course,' he admitted grimly, adding after a moment's silence, 'My main reason for telling you is because you'll need to be extra-vigilant.'

Peta shook her head, both fear and distress in her eyes. 'I'm not trained for this sort of thing; I don't know how to cope; I can't—'

'I know it's asking a lot of you,' he interrupted gently, almost afraid that he would scare her away, 'but I'm sure you'll look after Nikos as much as you do your own son. Your dedication to Ben, the way you put him before yourself at all times, is what made me think you'd be the ideal person to replace Bronwen. And now I'm even surer of it. Besides, Nikos adores you already. He'll do whatever you say. He doesn't know about this, of course, and I'd prefer it to remain that way. He's had all the usual warnings about going off with strangers, but nevertheless I still want you to be on your guard.'

For a moment he thought that Peta was going to refuse, that she was going to walk away; he could see by her scared expression that she felt her life would be in danger, too, and he saw the faint shudder that ran through her. 'I'm trusting you, Peta,' he said quietly but determinedly. 'Don't let me down.' To his disgust there was a break in his voice.

'It's a huge responsibility,' she whispered, 'I'm not sure I'm prepared to handle it, not even sure that I'm capable.'

He leaned forward again and took her hands into his. 'Let's hope it all comes to nothing,' he said gruffly, and, pulling her gently to her feet, he held her close.

Sensation ricocheted through Peta's body with the force of a speeding missile. Even the shock of hearing that Nikos was in danger had done nothing to diminish the feelings Andreas managed to arouse. It took every ounce of will-power and several deep breaths to calm herself and hide her catapulting emotions.

For a while he held her still, appearing to draw comfort, but then one hand began to slowly stroke the back of her head while the other, low on her back, urged her closer. His arousal was sudden and shocking.

She seemed to be living life on a seesaw. One moment believing herself safe, convinced that Andreas had no ulterior motives. The next fearful that he wanted her for only one thing. She couldn't let it happen.

'Let me go!' she muttered through her teeth. 'If you're after a lover as well as a child-minder and protector then you've made a grave mistake.'

'But you want me,' he murmured, his voice a low, sensual growl. 'Deny it if you can.'

How could she when he'd read her body signals so accurately? Not only today but last night as well. 'You're the sort of man most women would willingly go to bed with,' she admitted. 'You must be aware of that. But it doesn't mean that I will. I'm not in the market for an affair. I've vowed never to give my body freely again. The next time will be to the man I'm going to marry.'

'Honourable sentiments,' he said with a faint smile, 'but are you sure you can stick to them?'

In other words he was asking whether she was capable of ignoring her needs. Whether she was capable of ignoring *him*. Peta stiffened and pushed her hands against his chest, desperately trying to break free. But Andreas had other ideas.

His arm tightened; his hand slid from her hair to the side of her face to gently stroke, to send even deeper shivers of sensation through her. And then he tilted her chin and made her look up at him. Her first thought was that she must hide her emotions, make out that she was unaffected by his touch, until she saw the raw need mirrored in his eyes.

Quite how it happened she didn't know, but the next moment his mouth was on hers.

What had started off as a need to reassure Peta, to bolster his own spirits, was quickly snowballing out of control. The kiss was truly exciting, even more exciting than Andreas had imagined kissing Peta would be, yet he wasn't sure that he was doing the right thing. Peta James wasn't your average girl. She was as likely to slap him across the face as she was to kiss him back.

It was a risk he was prepared to take. For the last twenty-four hours she'd been driving him crazy. There was still the problem with Nikos, but this little minx even had the power to take his mind off that.

From the moment he'd caught her looking at him he had not stopped thinking about what it would be like to make love to her. And the fact that she had instantly denied her feelings had intrigued him even further. Despite the image she portrayed of being coolly in control of her life there burned beneath that outer shell a woman with a very real need.

Her mouth was as soft and sensual as he had imagined it would be. She tasted like the sweetest nectar, engaging every one of his senses, sending his mind whirling into orbit. He moved his lips gently at first, slowly increasing the pressure until he felt the early stirring of response.

Even heard it! Very softly, from somewhere deep in her throat, he heard a slight sound, a satisfied sound! Encouraged, he touched her sensitive lips with his

tongue, felt the ripple that ran through her, and when
her mouth moved restlessly beneath his he urged it open.

It was his turn to groan this time. He wanted to rush,
he wanted to plunder her mouth and take everything she
had to offer. He wanted to crush her to him; feel the
shape of her, explore, incite, demand. But even as these
urges burnt into him he knew that to do so would lose
him the one woman he trusted with his son's life.

He forced himself to slow down, to lessen the ur-
gency, to reluctantly end the kiss. And when he put her
from him he sensed that she was disappointed, too,
though none of it showed on her face.

Instead her beautiful sapphire eyes shot daggers across
the divide which a few minutes ago had been non-
existent and now felt a mile wide. She shivered and
hugged her arms across her body. 'What did you do that
for?' she asked crossly.

'Do what?' There was harshness in his voice also. She
made him feel as though he'd ravaged her against her
will and this didn't sit well on his shoulders.

'You know what,' she tossed. 'I need a promise from
you, Andreas. If I'm to stay on there will be no more
kisses. I don't want you to even touch me. It will completely ruin our working relationship—and that's all I'm
here for. Please remember that.'

She looked so fired-up and beautiful that it was all he
could do not to grab her and kiss her again. He hid his
desire behind hard, narrowed eyes. 'You didn't put up
much resistance.'

'Would it have done any good?' she questioned.

'I have never, in my life, taken anything from a
woman that she didn't want to give,' he declared shortly.
'You enjoyed it, Peta. Deny it if you like, but the proof
was there. I don't take kindly to being accused of using

force. If I were you I'd choose my words very carefully
the next time you feel like flinging accusations.'

He saw the way she gritted her teeth, the way her
fingers curled into her palms. But to give her credit her
voice was quietly calm as she spoke. 'I'd like to be
alone.'

When Andreas had gone Peta sank back into the chair
and closed her eyes. What had she done? Allowing him
to kiss her, not fighting back the instant he touched her,
must have given him all sorts of wrong ideas. One moment they'd been talking about kidnappers, the next
they'd been in a passionate clinch. How had that happened?

Hopefully, though, he was now convinced that she
held him totally responsible, that she was as angry as
hell and would walk out on the job if he dared try it
again. But would she? Hadn't that kiss aroused every
one of her senses? Didn't she want more?

The answer was painfully yes. And when Peta went
to bed later that evening she was still burning from his
touch. Her body felt as aroused now as it had when his
lips met hers.

She would have liked to think that it was because she
was hungry for a man, not this particular man, but any
man. Her mind knew, though, that this wasn't true.
She'd met plenty of men since Ben was born, and not a
single one had a lit a spark inside her.

So what did Andreas Papadakis have that these other
men hadn't? Was it because he was Greek? Because he
was darkly handsome? Because he was wealthy? Because of the authority that sat so well on his shoulders?
She didn't think it was any of these. It was an indefinable

something that would continue to puzzle her for the rest of her life.

Surprisingly sleep claimed her quickly, and this time, so that she wouldn't be late getting up, she set her alarm. The following morning she got Ben and Nikos ready and they ran downstairs to the warm kitchen, where Bess Middleton had breakfast ready. 'Mr Papadakis has already left,' she told Peta. 'Says to tell you that there's some work for you in his study. Any queries, you're to ring him.'

Peta nodded, but wondered why he hadn't told her himself last night. Except that they'd both had other things on their minds. Her skin went warm at the very thought of what had happened, but she was determined not to let it bother her. There would be no repeat, she had made that very clear. She would do the job she was getting paid for and ignore completely any foolish signs her body made.

When they left the house in the land-cruiser that Andreas insisted she use to ferry the boys around, she saw a black saloon parked a few yards from the entrance gates, the driver sitting reading a newspaper. It might be nothing, she reasoned—and yet again it could be extremely significant.

Fear prickled her skin and as she drove away Peta constantly checked her mirror. To her relief he didn't follow but she knew that it was imperative she constantly keep her wits about her, She wasn't happy until Nikos was safely within the school gates and she saw a teacher keeping a vigilant eye on all of the children.

The next few days followed a similar routine. Andreas always left her work to do, but he never came to her sitting room again. If he wanted to discuss anything he invited her into his study.

It didn't stop her being aware of his presence, however; she still felt a tingling awareness whenever he was close, and more than once she caught his eyes on her with such a hungry look that she needed to clench everything to stop giving herself away.

She saw the car a couple of times more and decided to tell Andreas. It might be nothing, it might be a rep having a five-minute break, killing time before his first appointment somewhere in the city, but better to be safe than sorry.

He nodded solemnly when she told him, his eyes narrowing. 'There could be a simple explanation—or it might be someone monitoring your movements. You got the registration number, I take it?'

'Yes.'

'Then I'll get it checked.' He looked at her gravely. 'You're not unduly worried? I don't want to stress you out, but Nikos's safety is, of course, my major concern.'

Peta nodded. 'I'm not frightened. I simply thought it odd seeing the car more than once.' In fact she thought he was taking this whole kidnap thing very calmly. If it were Ben in danger she'd be paranoid. She wouldn't let him out of her sight. She certainly wouldn't rely on someone else to look after him.

'If you're sure.' He closed the gap between them and put his arms around her. There was nothing sexual in the action this time; it was a simple, comforting gesture. Peta realised this as she buried her head in his shoulder. But it didn't stop the blood shooting hotly through her veins, or her pulses frantically leaping.

It was for only a brief moment. The next second she found herself free, and when she looked into his face there was nothing to suggest that he too had been affected. In fact his face was closed and hard and she guessed that he was worrying more about his son than he let on.

The next morning when she walked out to the landcruiser she found a note tucked behind the wiper blade. Her fingers shook as she opened it. 'SOON!' was all it said in bold black lettering, but she knew very well what it meant.

Andreas had already left, so she tucked the note quickly into her pocket before the boys saw, but her heart was in her mouth as she drove past the gates and looked for the black car. She intended getting a good look at the driver this time. It was almost a sense of anticlimax to find he wasn't there. Relief also, but it set her mind working.

When she gave Andreas the note that evening his face darkened. Muscles tightened in his jaw as he screwed the piece of paper up and tossed it into his wastebin. Almost immediately he realised what he'd done and fished it out again. 'The police will have to take it seriously now.'

He was back within the hour, his face tight with determination. 'Pack your bags,' he said tersely. 'We're leaving.'

CHAPTER FIVE

PETA looked at Andreas in wide-eyed shock. 'Leaving? At this hour?' The note must have scared him more than she'd thought. 'What did the police say?'

'They're checking fingerprints. And they'll take those of the owner of the black saloon—even though he's apparently a perfectly ordinary businessman. But I'm not leaving anything to chance. They took mine as well, and they want yours, but to hell with that. Go and get the boys ready.'

'But they're in bed,' she protested. 'It's unrealistic. A few more hours won't hurt, surely?'

Andreas drew in a deep breath, his hard-muscled chest rising. And then slowly, as he released it, some of the tension drained out of him. 'You're right,' he said, dragging a heavy hand through his hair. 'But we'll leave early tomorrow.'

Peta shook her head, still bemused by this sudden turn of events. 'Have the police suggested you move?'

'Hell, no. They're doing all they can. But I'm not leaving my son in danger any longer.'

'How about Linam's—your work there? Are you going to leave it to flounder?'

'Goodness, Peta, why all the questions? No, I am not. Within a few minutes I shall be on the phone, organising someone to step into my shoes. My younger brother, actually. He's very capable. I trust him completely.'

'So where are we going?'

'To Greece, of course.' He said it as though she was supposed to know.

'Greece?' she echoed shrilly.

'Yes, Greece,' he responded impatiently. 'Is that a problem for you?'

'Yes, it is, as a matter of fact. Ben doesn't have a passport. I got mine last year, when my mother insisted I take a holiday, but—'

'Then you'll have to leave him behind until he gets one.'

Peta couldn't believe he'd said that. She stared at him in wide-eyed horror and anger. 'I'm going nowhere without Ben,' she told him coldly.

Andreas clapped a hand to his brow. 'Forgive me. I spoke without thinking. I'll organise his passport first thing. You'd better get some sleep.'

It was impossible. Peta's mind was in a whirl. She couldn't quite take in the situation. It was all happening too quickly. Not that Ben would mind; he'd see it as a great adventure, especially as he'd have Nikos for company. Already he adored the other boy and they spent every minute together.

The next day, true to his word, Andreas sorted out Ben's passport and their schools and his own replacement. If she'd tried to do it she'd have come up against all sorts of red tape, but Andreas seemed to walk over everyone and get exactly what he wanted. This was Andreas Papadakis, action man. Not the seducer, not even the Tyrant, his mind was channelled on one thing only—getting his son away from the dangers that threatened. By the end of the day they were ready to go. 'First light we'll be on the move,' he announced.

*   *   *

Ben was awake before she was. He came bounding into her room, full of excitement. 'Wake up, Mummy. I want to go. I want to go now.'

In no time at all they were ready. Andreas drove to the airport, where he had his own jet fuelled up and waiting, but it was not until they were in the air that she saw him visibly relax. The smile came back to his face and he looked at her with a warmth that set her toes curling and her insides aflame.

'Thank you,' he said.

Her carefully shaped brows rose. 'For what?'

'For understanding, for obliging, for everything. You'll never know how much I appreciate it.'

'So long as Ben's OK then I am,' she declared with a slight shrug.

'That's how I feel about Nikos,' he admitted. 'I know I'm guilty of sometimes neglecting him, but I love him more dearly than life itself. If anything happened...' A dark shadow settled across his face.

He would have lost both his son and his wife, thought Peta. She wondered whether now would be a good time to ask how she had died. But Nikos spoke and the moment was lost.

She couldn't help thinking as she watched the boys playing with their pocket computer games that they looked like a family. Ben's hair wasn't as dark as Nikos's, but dark enough for them to pass as brothers. And anyone seeing her and Andreas with them could easily mistake them for husband and wife. It was an unreal situation.

When they arrived at Athens a car was waiting to whisk them swiftly away from the airport. Everything had been planned down to the last tiny detail. And they didn't have far to travel before the driver turned in through some magnificent iron gates and along a curving drive to a sprawling house which was every bit as palatial as the one they had left a few hours earlier. It had a red roof and white walls, and was built on several levels.

'My family home,' announced Andreas. 'We're expected.'

Even as they approached the central door opened and a dark-haired woman, probably in her late forties, stood waiting for the car to stop. She was dressed immaculately in a scarlet, black and white dress. Her nails were polished a similar red, her lips a slash of the same colour. She stood tall and proud with a haughty lift to her chin which Peta failed to recognise as one of her own particular stances.

She saw a strong resemblance and decided it was her boss's sister, at the same time acknowledging how little she knew about his family. She judged Andreas to be in his mid-thirties, and she'd just discovered he had a younger brother, now here was another family member. How many more were there?

She scrambled out of the car, calling Ben to stand by her, leaving Nikos to run across to the woman, who bent low and gathered him into her arms, smiling fondly as she did so. She greeted Andreas next; another wide smile and a hug, and a stream of Greek.

Then it was Peta and Ben's turn to be introduced. The woman looked at them with speculative eyes as they approached. No sign of a smile now. 'Peta,' said Andreas, 'I'd like you to meet my mother. Mother, this is Peta James, the girl I told you about, and this is Ben, her son.'

If a breath of wind had blown it would have knocked her over. This glamorous woman was Andreas's mother! She couldn't be; she wasn't old enough. Either she'd been a child bride or she was very adept at hiding her real age. Peta smiled faintly and held out her hand. It was taken reluctantly and limply, reinforcing Peta's impression that she wasn't welcome.

'So you are Nikos's nanny?' Her Greek was heavily accented. Brown eyes, so like her son's, looked coldly into hers. 'I hardly think he will have use for one here, but I have no doubt that we will be able to find something to keep you occupied.'

Peta's eyes flickered towards Andreas but he was busy talking to his son and gave no sign of having heard. She drew in a deep, steadying breath and held back a tart response. If she'd known they were going to be living with his parents she would have refused to come. She had, stupidly as it turned out, thought they'd be living alone, in Andreas's house, thought she would still be needed to look after Nikos.

'Come, let's go indoors,' Andreas said now. 'Stavros will see to our luggage.'

Inside the house was cool and airy. Mrs Papadakis clapped her hands and a young girl appeared on silent feet. She stood humbly in front of the older woman. 'Anna, please show the *despinis* to—'

'It's all right,' interrupted Andreas, 'I will take Peta myself. I'll join you in a minute, Mother.'

They walked what seemed like endless miles of corridor before entering, much to Peta's relief, a completely self-contained apartment. There was a well-sized living area, an enormous dining room, and a kitchen to die for. 'Mother's organised lunch today,' informed Andreas, 'but if my instructions have been carried out—' he peeked into a cavernous fridge and freezer '—which they have, there's everything we need here to be completely independent.'

Thank goodness, breathed Peta silently. The thought of joining his mother each mealtime was not a happy one.

On an upper floor her bedroom and Ben's were connected by a bathroom; big rooms, plenty of space for him to play. Andreas had his own suite, and Nikos's bathroom was next door to his room.

'I need to go and find my mother now,' Andreas said. 'Come and join us when you've freshened up.'

'If I don't get lost,' she warned. 'This place is huge.'

'You'll soon get used to it,' he said with a smile.

Peta nodded, even though she wasn't really sure.

Stavros brought up their cases, and after she'd unpacked Peta eventually found Andreas on the terrace, talking to his parent; Nikos was already in the pool.

'Oh, Mummy!' exclaimed Ben, his eyes wide and impressed. 'Can I go in?'

Andreas answered for her. 'But of course.'

Ben stripped down to his pants and jumped laughingly into the water to join his new friend. Peta watched him with an indulgent smile on her face. What an experience this was for him. And for her, too. Her life had completely turned around since she'd begun working for Andreas Papadakis. Who'd have thought a few short weeks ago that she'd be living here in this sun-drenched place with the man who had earned the reputation of being a tyrant? She was discovering that he was nothing of the sort. That he was a hot-blooded male who excited her beyond measure.

Andreas patted the seat beside him. 'Sit down. My mother wants to hear all about you.'

Peta bet she did. She was probably wondering whether she had any designs on her son, why he had brought a nanny all the way over from England when he could quite easily have found one here. And did he even need one when he had a doting grandmother to look after Nikos? Or wasn't Andreas's mother the maternal kind? She certainly didn't look it in her designer clothes and elegant sandals. It struck Peta that Mrs Papadakis was more interested in her own appearance than anything else.

'My son tells me that you are an unmarried mother,' were the woman's first words, a shudder of distaste running right through her pencil-slim body.

Peta lifted her chin proudly; she wasn't ashamed of it. 'Ben's lacked nothing because of it.'

'What happened to his father?'

'Mother, is this really necessary?' asked Andreas. 'It's none of our business.'

'I believe in the holy sanctimony of marriage,' declared the woman haughtily.

'It wasn't Peta's fault,' declared Andreas, with a warm smile in Peta's direction. 'In fact I think we can admire her for bringing up her son alone. He does her credit. And it's good for Nikos to have a companion.'

Peta felt a rush of warmth. She hadn't expected him to champion her.

'You should get married again, Andreas, and have more children of your own,' announced his mother.

And get rid of this woman who isn't necessary in your life. They were the unspoken words, decided Peta. His mother had for some reason taken an instant dislike to her. It was a wonder she was allowing her to sit with them, and if it wasn't for Andreas she probably wouldn't even be speaking to her now.

A faint bell sounded from somewhere in the interior of the house. 'Lunch is ready,' announced Andreas with some satisfaction. 'Come, Peta, you must be starving. Nikos, Ben, time to eat.'

The boys hauled themselves out of the pool, catching the towels Andreas tossed to them. 'Slip on your shirts, boys.'

Mrs Papadakis had already walked into the house, her back straight with disapproval, and Peta wasn't surprised when she didn't join them.

'I don't think your mother likes me,' she said when they had seated themselves at an oval table in a cool extension of the main kitchen.

'Since my father died my mother has found life very difficult,' he excused. 'In one respect it's her own fault because she doesn't make friends easily. Once she gets to know you she'll see what a wonderfully warm person you are. No one can help but fall for your charm, Peta.'

His eyes met and held hers. Peta felt her stomach turn over. What was he saying? That he wanted something more from their relationship? That the kiss had meant a whole lot more than she'd ever imagined? Her toes wriggled in her sandals and she fought to suppress the heat that was stealing over her skin. She didn't want a relationship with Andreas, not with anyone; she was happy as she was.

If that's the case, why did you come here? asked an inner voice. *You must have known what would happen.*

No, I didn't, she protested. I was merely helping him out.

To the extent that you gave up your home? Doesn't that tell you anything?

I felt sorry for Nikos.

Nikos? Rubbish! It's Andreas you're interested in, and the sooner you accept it the better.

Was her conscience right? Was she secretly hoping

for an affair? Or even something more? No! No! It couldn't be. She wouldn't let it. She didn't want a man in her life, not ever.

'Thank you for the compliment,' she said faintly. 'Time will tell.' And she turned to Ben. 'What would you like, darling?' The table was almost groaning under the weight of a splendid buffet lunch and soon the boys were chattering too much for them to hold a decent conversation.

Nevertheless she still felt Andreas's unsettling eyes on her more often than she would have liked. She really had thought that they'd come here to get away from the kidnap threats, not so that Andreas could make a pass at her.

Unfortunately the thought was tremendously exciting, and if she wasn't careful it would be revealed in her eyes. Deliberately now she kept her gaze on the table, or the boys, trying not to look at Andreas even when he spoke to her.

As soon as they'd finished eating Nikos and Ben wanted to go back into the pool, but Andreas forbade them until their lunch had gone down. 'Go and play football, but mind Nana's prized plants or you'll be in trouble.'

Peta said, 'I think I'll go and supervise.' Anything to get away from Andreas and the sensual signals he was sending out.

But Andreas had other ideas. 'Leave them. I want to talk.'

About what? Nikos? His mother? Or their own relationship? Her heart skittered along at an amazing pace.

'I'm worried about Nikos's education while we're out here. I don't want to send him to school because he's an easy target if—'

'You don't think that whoever's threatened to kidnap your son knows you've moved here?' she asked in horror.

'Of course not, but I'm not giving anyone a chance. I could bring in a private tutor for both boys, but I was wondering what you'd think about doing the job?'

Peta burst out laughing. 'From PA to nanny, to tutor. You must think I'm a many-talented person.'

'I have every faith in you.'

'Then you're mistaken. I can't teach, I don't know the first thing about it.'

'You're good at English and maths. And I'm sure you know enough about history and geography to teach a seven- and eight-year-old. I think you're eminently qualified. And what you don't know I do. I'll get all the relevant books and together we'll make a good team.'

Together!

It was the way he said it that filled her with foreboding. They were not a team, she didn't want to be a team. All the time he was adding to her list of responsibilities and now he was including himself in her duties. It wasn't on. This wasn't part of the original score.

'You don't look happy about it.'

'I'm not,' she flashed. 'If I'd known what was in store I wouldn't have come. I thought you'd be busy all day and every day and that I'd look after Ben and Nikos. I didn't even expect to be living with your mother. I assumed you had your own villa.'

He gave a typically foreign shrug. 'I sold it. I saw no point in keeping it on when I'm here so infrequently. Besides, when I do come over I feel obliged to spend time with my mother. And to check up on my inheritance, of course,' he added with a wry grin. 'I'm sorry you feel that way.'

'The whole situation is growing out of all proportion,' she argued.

'I want you to have a good time,' he said softly.

She raised her brows then and looked at him. 'This isn't a holiday.'

'No, but I don't want it to be onerous, I want you to enjoy it. Naturally there are things I need to do, I have to keep up with my business interests, but I want to spend time with Nikos as well.'

He hadn't done very much of that so far, thought Peta. Had it taken a kidnap threat to make him realise how important Nikos was to him? She couldn't understand the man. Ben was everything to her, always had been, always would be. She would never have neglected him the way Andreas neglected Nikos.

He stood now and moved to stand behind her. He touched his hands to her shoulders and she went tense. Instead of moving he began to massage.

Peta felt a deep heat invade her body and she wanted to jump up and run away before it took hold, but to do so would reveal too much about her feelings. She sat as still as a fawn caught in a car's headlights, not even breathing, hoping that he'd get the message and go away.

What was it going to take, Andreas wondered, to get Peta to relax with him? She was driving him crazy. He'd thought that she'd enjoy new sights and sounds, forget her animosity towards men in general and allow him into her life.

Nothing seemed further from her mind.

'I'm serious about wanting you to enjoy your time here, Peta,' he said, continuing to massage slowly and surely until he felt the tension start to drain out of her.

'It's not supposed to be all work and no play. We'll go sightseeing, we'll do all sorts of things together—the four of us.' The last was added when he felt her stiffen again, when he knew she was thinking that he'd meant just the two of them. Which he had!

He increased the pressure, massaging deeper and deeper, feeling great pleasure as she gradually relaxed. Her closeness intoxicated him, sent a lightness to his head as though he'd drunk an expensive wine. He felt himself swaying closer towards her, inhaling the heady fragrance of her perfume, hearing her faint murmurs of satisfaction. He became so engrossed in what he was doing, in the feel and smell of this exciting girl who was becoming such an important part of his life, that he didn't hear his mother enter the room.

'Andreas!' she rapped.

He felt Peta jump, felt the tension return with a vengeance and cursed his parent for intruding at this particular moment. With one word she had undone all that he'd achieved.

With a slow smile and no sign of embarrassment Andreas turned to his mother. Peta, on the other hand, felt mortified. If the woman hadn't thought it before she must surely now be convinced that she was trying to latch on to her son.

'You want something, Mother?'

Dark eyes flashed contemptuously in Peta's direction, and then back to her son. 'A little of your time, *if* you can spare it.'

Peta pushed herself to her feet, standing tall and proud, not letting this objectionable woman see for one second that she was disturbed by her presence. 'I'll go and find the boys,' she said pleasantly.

But outside she stood and fumed. She could see now where Andreas's autocracy came from. Except that somewhere deep inside him lived a warm, generous, compassionate human being. She doubted many people saw it. Maybe that part came from his father. Or was she misjudging his elegant mother? Was there warmth inside her, too? If so it was well-hidden.

She found Ben and Nikos kicking a ball around on one of the terraces, but they soon tired of it and begged to be allowed in the pool again. Peta decided to join them. But on her way up to her room to change she bumped into Andreas's mother.

The woman looked at her down the length of her nose. 'A word with you, please.'

Peta smiled carefully, doing her best to hide her inner tension.

'Follow me.'

She was taken to what Peta presumed was her own private sitting room. The walls were a yellow-ochre colour, and the easy chairs and cream leather settee sat on a square of carpet patterned in the same yellow, with splashes of sage-green and ivory. The rest of the floor was tiled in cream. In her scarlet, black and white outfit, the older woman stood out like a blot of red wine on a white tablecloth.

Mrs Papadakis carefully shut the door behind them and whirled to confront Peta. 'Tell me exactly why you are here.' The red slash of her lips was tight and straight, her dark brown eyes filled with suspicion.

'I think you already know.' Peta tried to keep her tone pleasant as she boldly looked the older woman in the eye, but it was difficult keeping it up in the face of such animosity.

'You are posing as Nikos's nanny, I believe. It is actually my son you are interested in, is that not so?'

Peta shook her head vigorously. 'Andreas hired me to look after Nikos. It wasn't my idea.'

'You were previously his personal assistant?'

'Yes.'

'You have no training in looking after children?'

'Not exactly, no paper qualifications, but I have Ben. I understand children and I love them. I—'

'And you are also in love with my son. Is that not so?'

'No!' Peta's response was immediate. 'Most definitely not.'

'It does not look that way to me. Let us get this straight here and now, Miss Peta James, you are not good enough for my Andreas. He will marry no woman who has a child out of wedlock; I will see to that. Besides, he is still in love with Maria.'

Peta felt a slither of discomfort. Who the hell was Maria?

Fine black brows rose. 'He has not told you about her? Maria was his wife. He loved her deeply. He went completely to pieces when she died. I doubt anyone will ever take her place.'

'I see,' said Peta quietly. 'But it makes no difference. Ours is purely a business arrangement.'

'Then why was he touching you?' asked Mrs Papadakis fiercely. 'You—you had your eyes closed and such a look of pleasure on your face that it was positively sickening.'

Oh, Lord! It was true, she had enjoyed his touch, it had created sensations that she'd rather not remember, but for his mother to have witnessed it was excruciatingly embarrassing. 'The pleasure was in having the tension in my shoulders relieved,' she announced primly.

'And why were you tense, may I ask?'

'I was up early, it's been a long day, everything's new.' And your less-than-warm welcome didn't help, she added silently. 'I worry too whether Ben will like it here. There are a hundred and one reasons.'

'And not one of them concerns my son?'

'Why should it?' asked Peta boldly. 'You're very much mistaken, Mrs Papadakis, in thinking that I'm interested in Andreas for any other reason than that he's paying my wages.'

'You do not find him remotely attractive?'

What the devil was his mother trying to do? Did she want her to say that she was angling after an affair with him? That he was a good catch and his money would be useful? Would that satisfy her? The answer was undoubtedly yes. It was the very ammunition Mrs Papadakis needed to throw her out.

'I think any woman would find your son attractive,' she said with her head held high, her blue eyes looking directly into the other woman's. 'He's not the sort of man you can dismiss easily. But I can assure you there's nothing going on between us, nor is there likely to be. I have no intention of getting involved with a man again, ever.'

She crossed her fingers behind her back, because if there was one man who could make her change her mind it was Andreas Papadakis. He had lit fires inside her that had taken her completely by surprise and she was having to fight every one of her self-imposed rules.

'Good,' came the swift response. 'I am glad to hear it. You may go now.'

The woman's tone set Peta's hackles rising; she was

treating her like a servant, like one of her own employees. About to open her mouth and ask who the hell she thought she was talking to, Peta had second thoughts. This was Andreas's mother, and if she wanted to keep her job then she'd better respect her.

She swung on her heel without another word, but was fuming as she made her way to their apartment. Did Andreas's mother ever come here? she wondered as she closed the connecting door. Or were these rooms sacrosanct? Were they totally Andreas's domain? She hoped with all her heart that it was so.

After changing swiftly into a swimsuit with a matching overshirt, Peta hurried back out and flung herself into the pool. She did several punishing lengths before she began to calm down, ignoring the cries of the boys as they tried to attract her attention.

It was Andreas who eventually stopped her, cutting in front and forcing her to slow down. 'What's wrong?' he asked. 'You look as though you're ridding yourself of demons.'

He urged her to the side, where they hauled themselves up and sat on the edge with their feet dangling in the water. He had an incredible body, she discovered, all hard muscle and deeply tanned skin. It did nothing for her equilibrium. It sent all sorts of indecent thoughts rushing through her mind.

'Maybe I was,' she mumbled, then corrected herself. 'I was in need of some exercise.'

'I see,' he said quietly, but she could see that he didn't. It was there in the frown that creased his handsome forehead, in the puzzled look. 'Has my mother said something to upset you?'

'Why should she?' asked Peta, not looking at him, watching her toes instead as she swished them in the water. She didn't want him to say anything to his parent, she didn't want the woman to think she had been telling tales.

'I know what she's like.'

Peta shook her head. 'It's not your mother. Like I said, I've been sitting all day; I needed to wake up my body. Having a pool of your own is the height of luxury as far as I'm concerned. Ben loves it already.' The boys were racing up and down the pool now, each one trying to outdo the other.

'There are other ways I could wake up your body.'

He spoke softly, and Peta thought she must have misheard, but when she glanced at him she knew differently. There was a burning light in his eyes and it sent a shiver down her spine. She looked away again quickly, pretended she hadn't heard, hadn't seen. 'Isn't it good the way Ben and Nikos get on together?'

'Mmm.' It was an abstracted sound, as though he hadn't been listening. He continued to look at her in that mind-burning way.

Even though his mother was probably right and his heart did belong to Maria, thought Peta, it didn't stop him wanting, perhaps needing a woman in his bed. And maybe that was what she wanted, too. Would an affair with him be such a bad thing? At least she would know from the onset that at the end of it they would each walk away with their hearts intact. But it was a big decision to make. She needed to consider it.

'I think I might join them again,' she said huskily, in an effort to delay the moment.

'No, Peta, wait.' His hand touched her arm and Peta knew that if she dived into the pool now she'd be electrocuted. Such a jolt had shot through her at his touch that it was all she could do not to snatch away. 'Why is it that you're afraid of me?' he asked quietly.

She attempted a laugh, but it came out as a hollow sound with no semblance of laughter. 'What are you saying? Why should I be scared of you?'

'You tell me.' He touched her chin and turned her face to him. 'I think we're both aware of a mutual attraction, so why fight it?'

'Because it wouldn't be proper,' she burst out breathlessly. 'I'm in your employ. Are you forgetting that? There's a world of difference between our lifestyles.'

'I couldn't give a damn,' he exploded. 'Barriers don't exist where need is concerned. I know you've been hurt, I know that you've sheathed yourself in ice so that no man can touch you again, but something tells me that the time has come for the ice to melt. In fact I think it's already melted a little. Am I right?'

Peta closed her eyes, wincing inwardly. He was so very near the mark. And before she could say anything he said, 'The fact that you're not denying it tells me all I need to know.'

'You think you're so clever, don't you?' Sharp words were her only form of defence. 'You think every girl you come into contact with falls for your charm. I don't want an affair with you, Andreas. If and when I ever fall in love again it will be all or nothing. I have no time for casual sex.'

She flattened her feet against the side of the pool, ready to dive back into the water, but Andreas, guessing her intention, reached an arm out as a barrier—and then he kissed her. Right there in front of the boys.

CHAPTER SIX

THE kiss lasted no more than a few seconds, but it was enough to tell Peta that the dam had broken and feelings and sensations such as she had never experienced before were flooding in. She wanted to cling, she wanted to kiss him again; she wanted to take all he had to offer.

And Andreas saw it. He saw the colour that flushed her cheeks, he saw the passion that darkened her eyes, and he saw the battle she had with herself.

'It's all right,' he murmured. 'It's all right to let go.'

She searched his face, looking anywhere except into his eyes because she knew that if she did she would be lost. But it was just as bad looking at his mouth, at those beautifully moulded lips that seconds ago had claimed hers. Unconsciously the tip of her tongue came out to moisten her own lips and she heard his warning groan before he leaned forward and took her mouth again.

His arms didn't hold her, she was as free as a bird, but it felt as if she was his prisoner. It felt as if his mouth was shackling her to him and there was no escape. It was telling her that this was what she wanted, needed, had been looking for ever since Joe let her down.

'Mummy!'

The spell was broken, and as she moved her head Peta saw out of the corner of her eye Andreas's mother watching them from an upstairs window. The pleasure of the moment faded, unease taking its place. This woman had the power to make her life here very uncomfortable, and she had unfortunately just given her the ammunition.

The water was blessedly cool as she launched herself in, and for the next half an hour she and Andreas played with the boys. It felt good, it felt as if they were a real family, and if it hadn't been for his disapproving parent Peta would have felt happier than she had in her whole life.

Parents were always reluctant to let go, she realised, even when you were grown up and capable of making your own decisions. Andreas's mother didn't want to accept that he was getting on with his life after Maria. And her own mother, when she'd phoned to tell her first of all that she was moving in with her employer, and then actually going to live in Greece with him, had been totally against it.

The fact that Peta hadn't had time to go and see her mother and father before leaving England had put her even deeper into their bad books. Of course, Peta hadn't told them about the kidnap threats for fear of worrying them further, and so her mother had immediately drawn her own conclusions. 'You won't be happy with a man like that,' she'd warned. 'Money doesn't bring happiness. It'll be a five-minute wonder and then where will you be? Really, Peta, at your age you should have more sense.'

Peta and Andreas tired before the boys did, stepping out of the pool and throwing themselves down on a couple of sun loungers. Here, the umbrellas hid them from the house; not that Peta had any intention of letting Andreas kiss her again. She must remember at all times that this was a job, that she wasn't here to indulge in anything sexual; she was here to look after Nikos.

The thought had her springing to her feet. If that was

the case, why was she lying here at all? No wonder his mother had drawn erroneous conclusions. The signals they gave off told entirely the wrong story.

It was Andreas's fault. If he'd remained the difficult tyrant none of this would have happened; if he'd remained aloof, if he hadn't insisted she call him Andreas. Now she was in danger of making a fool of herself.

'Where are you going?'

Peta turned reluctantly at the sound of his voice. He had pushed himself up on one elbow, a sharp frown etching his brow.

'I shouldn't be doing this,' she told him shortly. 'I'm forgetting my position. I'm going to shower and get changed.' And before he could say anything else Peta hurried towards the house.

Andreas was sorry to see Peta go. For the first time he had felt she was beginning to relax with him, really relax, and when he'd kissed her he could have sworn that she was enjoying it. He had wanted the kiss to go on and on, he had wanted more of her, everything, all! But knew he still had to tread carefully. And now it looked as though even that brief kiss had frightened her off again.

He lay back and closed his eyes. He listened to the boys shouting and laughing, and then he heard the click of footsteps coming towards him. Peta? She had dressed already, was back into the nanny role he had created for her.

Little had he known when he'd asked her to look after Nikos that he would fall under her spell. She was so very different from Maria, who had used her sex appeal to its full. It was what had enchanted him about her. He had loved it when she'd turned other men's heads with her sultry looks and swaying hips, loved the fact that she'd wanted no one but him. He'd been devastated when she died.

Peta appealed to him in an entirely different way. She had no artifices. What you saw was what you got. He had thought he would never love again, would never find anyone to capture his heart. He wasn't even sure that Peta had done that. He wanted her physically, yes—she drove him crazy in that respect—but did he want more? Of that he wasn't sure.

'Andreas,' said a voice in Greek, 'I need to talk to you.'

Damn, it was his mother. His train of thought vanished as he sat up. 'Couldn't it have waited?'

'No, it couldn't,' she said with some asperity. 'It's about Peta James.'

His eyes sharpened. He had picked up on the fact that his mother didn't approve, and now she was here to voice her opinion. 'What about her?'

The older woman sat gingerly on the edge of the lounger Peta had vacated. 'She's far too familiar with you, for one thing.'

Andreas allowed his brows to slide upwards. 'Mother, you're living in the wrong era. She might be Nikos's nanny, but that's no excuse for me to treat her like a servant.'

'I saw you kissing her,' she snapped. 'She told me there was nothing between you. I knew she was lying.'

'You've spoken to her about me?' he barked, swift anger beginning to rise. Now he knew why Peta had looked worried, why she had suddenly run away. 'You had no right.'

'I have every right,' she thrust back. 'I have no desire

to see a son of mine make a fool of himself over a girl who is entirely unsuitable.'

'And you think that's what I'm doing?'

'Is it not?'

'If you'd get to know Peta better then you'd know differently,' he retorted. 'She has integrity, intelligence, is an excellent mother, and what's more is the first girl I've been interested in since Maria died.'

'Are you saying that you no longer are in love with Maria?'

'In my memories I'll always love her,' he admitted with a hint of sadness, 'but life has to go on.'

'For me there will never be anyone but your father.'

'You had a long time together,' he pointed out. 'Maria and I had a few years. I have my whole life in front of me, I don't intend spending it alone.'

'Then for pity's sake find someone more suitable than that English girl. You are Greek, Andreas, are you forgetting that? You should marry someone from your homeland.'

'I've not said I'm going to marry Peta,' he insisted. 'Although now you've put the idea in my head it might not be such a bad thing.'

His mother shook her head in despair. 'Don't do this to me, Andreas.'

'There are some things over which a mother has no control,' he said to her gently. 'And her son falling in love is one of them.'

'So you do love her?' she accused.

'I haven't said that. I find her immensely attractive, but so far it's gone no further. And I'd appreciate it if you didn't frighten her off by threats.'

His mother clamped her lips; it was obvious she was having difficulty in holding back a further tirade. In the end she simply shook her head and walked swiftly back to the house.

Andreas didn't see Peta again until he found her sitting with the boys while they ate the supper she had prepared.

He joined her in the window-seat, keeping his voice low so that Nikos and Ben couldn't hear. 'My mother had no right speaking to you as she did. Oh, yes, I know all about it,' he added when she looked at him in surprise. 'She tried to get to me, too.' He smiled indulgently. 'She still thinks she can tell me what to do. I think it's because she has too much time on her hands. She's lonely, and she'd love me to move back here permanently.'

'How about your brother? Does he live at home?'

'What do you think?' he asked with a devilish grin. 'Neither of us could wait to move out. We loved our parents dearly but there comes a time when a man needs his own space.'

'Is Christos married?'

'No.'

It was Peta's turn to give an impish smile. 'Perhaps he'll find a nice English girl to settle down with.'

'And upset my mother altogether?' he said with a laugh. 'Poor dear, she really does live in another age. But let's not talk about her any more; let's talk about us.' He saw the startled light in her eyes, knew she wanted to move away, so he reached out and took her hand. 'You can't ignore the spark that exists.' Even now it was sending an army of sensations through his loins.

'I can and I do,' she told him heatedly. 'There can be nothing between us, Andreas. It's crazy even thinking about it. I didn't take the job because I wanted an affair.

I took it because I felt sorry for Nikos. He is my main responsibility.'

So he meant nothing to her. Andreas felt personally affronted. It hadn't felt like nothing when he kissed her, he was sure she had been equally aroused. So why was she denying it?

Peta knew she was right in declaring that she was here to do a job and nothing else. No matter what thoughts, what emotions, what sensations ran through her, she had to ignore them.

Andreas wasn't in love with her; he simply lusted after her. She had read it in his eyes, seen it in the way he looked at her, felt it in his kiss. It had done all sorts of things to her that should never have been allowed, but what was the point in indulging in an affair? His world was a far cry from hers. For all she knew he could have had a string of girlfriends since he'd lost Maria.

'What are you thinking?'

She looked at him then, saw that he was watching her, that his eyes were as dark as a midnight sky.

'I was listening to the boys.' Ben and Nikos were squabbling, she suddenly realised. It gave her the perfect excuse.

'Liar.' It was a gentle reproval, there was even the hint of a smile. 'You were thinking about us. Deny it if you dare.'

Peta shrugged her slender shoulders. 'Maybe I was. Maybe I was realising what a big mistake I've made.'

The smile changed to a frown. 'In letting me kiss you?' There was a faint edge to his tone this time.

'It wasn't the right thing to do, especially with your mother watching. Rest assured, it won't happen again.'

'In that case,' he said with a wicked smile, 'we'll have to be more careful.'

'There won't be another time,' Peta assured him sharply.

The grin widened. 'What if you can't help yourself?'

'I shall make sure I don't put myself in such a position,' she announced haughtily. 'Ben, stop that, will you?'

'Are you making a point here? Reminding me that it's the boys you're here to supervise? That I am a no-go area?'

She nodded. 'Exactly.'

'I think you might find that very difficult.' He sat more comfortably in his seat, looking wholly amused by the whole conversation. 'I think maybe you don't realise the strength of your own feelings.'

'And I think maybe you are seeing things that aren't there,' she retorted sharply, and, turning her head, said, 'Boys, will you please stop arguing?'

When they realised they were being observed Ben and Nikos shut up and got on with their meal.

'We'll finish this conversation later,' said Andreas, finally accepting that he was getting nowhere while the boys were present. Lazily he pushed himself up, but his eyes never left her. They stroked intimately over her whole body—arousing, hurting, even, sending sensation after sensation sizzling through her veins.

Peta closed her eyes until he had left the room. She didn't want to see, didn't want to feel. It had been a mistake coming here to Greece with Andreas and his son. She had thought they would all get on together, that it would be a good experience for Ben, but Andreas was spoiling it. He was asking far more of her than she was prepared to give.

Had it been his intention all along? Was that the reason he'd insisted she change her job? He'd virtually given her no choice; she would have been out of work altogether if she hadn't gone along with his request. And now she was in the unenviable position of allowing herself to be seduced by him or being shipped back to England without a job or a home to go to. There was always her mother, of course, but...

An hour later, when the boys were in bed and Peta was sitting out on the living-room balcony, enjoying the last rays of the sun which had turned the sky above Athens into a glowing red furnace, she sensed rather than saw Andreas standing beside her.

She hadn't been aware of him approaching, miles away with her thoughts, and now she looked at him in surprise and not without a little trepidation. She had been thinking about their conversation, about the way her body reacted when he was near, and whether she was being foolish denying herself the pleasure she knew he could give her. He was aware, of course, exactly how she felt, and if he put the pressure on she would be lost. But where would it get them? It would surely be better to maintain a safe distance, to do the job she had been brought out here for, and to hell with anything else.

'Aren't you hungry?' The words meant one thing, his eyes another.

Peta felt a stinging sensation hit the very core of her. Damn him! 'I wasn't sure whether you were. I didn't know what you expected of me.' In truth food was the furthest thought from her mind.

'Actually, I'm starving,' he said 'You stay here and enjoy all these new sights and sounds. I'll rustle us both up something to eat.'

'You cook?' she enquired. This was a surprise, coming from a man who could afford an army of servants.

'You think I can't?'

Peta turned her lips down at the corners and shrugged. 'I've never really thought about it.'

'But you think I'm spoilt and pampered, unable to lift a finger for myself?' There was a twinkle in his eyes as he spoke.

'You said it,' she retorted with a grin.

'There are lots of things about me you don't know,' he told her. 'Be prepared for a culinary delight. Maybe madam would like a glass of wine while she's waiting?'

'Maybe madam doesn't drink.'

'Of course. I was forgetting. A fruit juice, then? Something long and cold and inviting?' His voice went down an octave, becoming suddenly seductive and exciting.

Peta gave a faint smile and nodded. 'That would be nice.' And her stomach did a somersault, which didn't bode well for an intimate evening spent together. Maybe there would have been something welcome about his mother being present after all.

It seemed that no time had elapsed before he announced that dinner was ready.

He'd laid the table with an ornately embroidered tablecloth and heavily engraved silver.

'It looks very formal for a simple supper,' she said doubtfully.

'The man wants to impress the lady.'

'I'll reserve judgement until I've eaten,' she answered.

He pulled out her chair, his hands dropping to her shoulders as she sat. Nothing more than a fleeting touch, but it was enough to send all her good intentions crashing to the floor.

The food was simple but superbly cooked: melon to start with, followed by chicken breasts in a delicious tomato sauce served with potatoes that had been braised in the same sauce. Peta wasn't sure how she got through it; she was aware of nothing but Andreas and the power he exerted over her. Power was a strange word to use, she thought. Andreas was a powerful man in the business world, he had a powerful body, too, but this was power of a different kind.

It was a silent, insidious power; power over her body. He was taking her over whether she wanted him to or not. It was a mind game. He was playing with her emotions, making her want him against her will.

They talked about all sorts of things while they ate— the state of the world, the state of the company back in England, the boys—anything and everything except themselves. But Peta thought that now might be a good time to ask him about Maria.

Here, in this apartment, she could feel her presence, feel an invisible third party. There was a portrait hanging on the upstairs landing of a beautiful young woman with jet-black hair and flashing dark eyes that followed her whenever she walked past. She guessed it was his wife because Nikos looked so very much like her.

'Yes, that's Maria,' Andreas admitted, when Peta dared to ask, and she saw the inevitable sadness in his eyes. It looked to her as though Maria's ghost would haunt him for ever.

'Did you live here when you were married?' she asked as she took a sip of her coffee, unable to think of any other reason for his wife's portrait to be here.

'Not until my father became ill and Mother couldn't manage. He was sick for a long time. And after he'd died my mother needed me more than ever.'

So that was the reason his parent was so possessive, thought Peta. 'Did it work?' she asked. 'Did Maria mind?'

'She loved it because she had company while I was out at work. I worked very long hours,' he admitted with a surprising touch of guilt. 'She and my mother got on well. Maria was the daughter of an old friend of my parents. I'd known her practically all my life. And when Nikos came along it was exactly what my mother needed to give her a new lease of life. There was no thought then of us moving out.'

'How long since Maria died?' Peta asked gently, feeling nothing but sympathy for this man who clearly still had very deep feelings for the woman who had borne him his son.

He drew in a slow, deep breath. 'Two years, almost. It was a tragic, tragic day.' His mind seemed to go back in time and it was several long seconds before he spoke again. 'It was a road accident. Nikos was with her. For some reason Maria didn't have her seat belt on; she stood no chance. Nikos was strapped in but he can remember nothing of it. I think the accident traumatised him to such an extent that he's blocked it out. If I ever catch the swine who drove her off the road I'll kill him,' he announced fiercely. 'It's a notorious bend, with a sheer drop, but Maria knew that road well, always took care.'

'So the police never traced the other car?'

'No. There was red paint on her car, so we know someone else was involved, but who it was will always remain a mystery. I sure hope whoever it was has it on his conscience for the rest of his life,' he finished bitterly.

'I'm so sorry,' said Peta. 'You must have been devastated.'

'To put it mildly,' he agreed. 'I blame myself entirely. I'd planned to take Maria and Nikos out that day, then something cropped up at work and as usual I refused to delegate. We had a row; she said I always put work before her.' He dropped his head, pressing his fingers to throbbing temples. 'And dammit she was right. I did. I do. I threw myself into my work more than ever after she died. And poor Nikos. I couldn't bear to have him around me. He's so like Maria that it was torture every time I looked at him. I didn't think the pain would ever go away.'

'It's all right,' said Peta softly. 'You don't have to tell me any more.' Because suddenly she understood. 'It's not an easy thing to get over.'

'I'm getting there,' he announced, finally lifting his head. 'And there's a certain beautiful young lady who's proving to me that there is life after Maria.' The look in his eyes said it all.

Peta tried to look away but couldn't. Their eyes locked in a heart-stopping moment that sent the blood screaming through her veins. 'We can't get involved,' she whispered.

'You tell me why not, when we both know it's what we want.'

The tension between them increased. 'You know why,' she managed to say.

'They're not valid reasons.'

'They are as far as I'm concerned,' she insisted.

'Then we need to do something about changing your mind. Let's get out of here; let's go for a walk.'

'But the boys...' It was a meek protest.

'They won't wake; you know that. You're looking for excuses.'

It was true. The next few minutes were going to be the turning point in their relationship. There would be no going back. Was she prepared for an affair that could lead nowhere? Would she be able to walk away at the end of it with her heart whole?

Night had fallen and mood lights were on in the pool and grounds, giving the whole place a magical air. Andreas put his arm about her shoulders as they walked, keeping her close to him, saying nothing, but his very silence sent its own message.

Peta knew deep down in her mind that she could fight him no longer, and when they were out of sight of the house, when he halted, when he turned her to face him, she gave a brief sigh of capitulation. The noise of cicadas filled the air, the heat of the day lingered, and the sky had become a canopy of shimmering stars.

Andreas stroked her cheek with the backs of his fingers and murmured something in Greek. He pulled down her lower lip and dropped a light kiss onto it; he urged her against him, and when she didn't demur, when she didn't back away, he gave a sigh of his own before claiming her lips.

Gently, experimentally—testing, waiting—wanting, needing. Peta's body grew hot, every nerve-end so sensitised that the briefest touch aroused her and evoked a need that shocked and thrilled at the same time. She returned his kiss with an amazed abandonment. It felt like release from a prison of her own making. A glorious release that had her soaring with the angels.

Andreas's groan of pleasure came from somewhere deep in his throat and his arms tightened, his kiss became deeper, his tongue touching hers now, exploring, inciting, taking everything that she offered. They suddenly couldn't get enough of each other. The floodgates had opened and their pent-up emotions were in full flow.

Only once did he hold back. 'You are sure?' he questioned, his voice deeper than she had ever heard it before.

Her response was a whimper of pleasure, her mouth reaching for his again.

Once more a flood of Greek. He was the most exciting man she had ever met. All the weeks she had known him she had been aware of his raw sensuality, but to feel it now, to taste him, to share the intimacy of mindless kisses when senses took over and the outer world was forgotten, was like nothing she had ever imagined or experienced.

How long the kiss went on Peta wasn't sure. Her mind had ceased to register anything except the thrill of kissing Andreas, the sheer headiness of having his body pressed close against hers. All barriers were down, they were existing on sensations alone, each drinking the sweet nectar of life from each other's mouths.

It was an extraordinary feeling. She had never, in her wildest imaginings, envisaged that she would kiss Andreas Papadakis, especially like this. He was the Tyrant. He was her boss. He was far beyond her reach.

'If I don't stop now—' his mouth edged away from hers, and his hoarse voice reached into her consciousness '—I won't be responsible for my actions.'

Nor would she, Peta realised, even as he kissed her again. She didn't want him to stop; she didn't want him to be responsible. She wanted everything he had to offer.

'You have no idea what you're doing to me,' he groaned.

Oh, yes, she had. If the kiss was affecting him half as

much as it was her then she knew exactly how he was feeling. His whole body would be on fire, his every instinct would be to make love to her, to drown in her body, to enjoy, to take everything that was willingly offered.

'Oh, Peta,' he muttered. 'I never dreamt that…'

He was robbed of the rest of his sentence by Peta's hungry mouth taking his. 'I know how you're feeling,' she whispered between passionate kisses, 'because I feel the same way.'

His answer was an even deeper groan, one hand moving to possessively capture an already swollen and tingling breast. A fresh surge of emotions coursed through her, an even greater need to be taken completely, and when Andreas let her go, when he stepped back a pace and looked at her with a mixture of sorrow and desire, she felt as though part of her had been snatched away.

'We need to take things slowly,' he said, shaking his head. He didn't sound as though he meant it. He sounded as though the words were being forced out of him by a hidden source.

That same hidden source had Peta agreeing with him. 'I don't know what came over me.' And as she thought about it a rich tide of colour stained her neck and face. To hide her embarrassment she turned from him and headed back towards the house.

'Peta!'

It was a command and she instinctively obeyed, halting but not turning, waiting but not wanting. This was all wrong. It could lead nowhere, could end only in disaster.

'Don't run away from me.' His voice got nearer. 'We both got carried away.' He was standing right behind her. She could feel his breath warm on her nape even though he was very carefully not touching her.

'It shouldn't have happened,' she whispered sadly.

'Oh, yes, it should,' he muttered thickly. 'It was a very natural, a very right thing to do. We both wanted it, we both needed it, and you can't walk away from me now.'

'But—'

'But nothing. You can't ignore your feelings, Peta.'

'I must,' she declared, finally turning to face him, and then wishing she hadn't when her eyes met his and she felt herself being drawn once more into their dark, disturbing depths. Why, oh, why had she agreed to come out here? she asked herself. For all these years she'd religiously kept men out of her life, and now, when she was least expecting it, she had fallen hook, line and sinker for a man who wanted nothing more from her than a brief affair.

'Why must you?' He put his hands on her shoulders and looked even more deeply into her eyes. 'Why not enjoy yourself while you can? I promise I won't hold you to anything. You'll be free to walk away whenever you like.'

The fact that he was saying what she already knew made Peta even more determined not to let herself get swept along on an unstoppable tide of passion. 'And you think I'd be happy doing that?' she tossed sharply. 'I'm not the type of girl to indulge in a passionate affair and then walk away. I can't even think why I let you kiss me.'

'Because you couldn't help yourself, the same as I couldn't. So why deny ourselves what we both want?'

'But I don't want it,' she flashed. 'I couldn't help kissing you, but I didn't want to do it.'

'You're not making sense, Peta.' His hands tightened on her shoulders, his eyes compelled her to look at him.

'Maybe not,' she agreed. 'But I don't want to start anything I can't finish. We both know that we're not into serious relationships. So for goodness' sake, Andreas, let this thing drop.'

His voice became a deep, throaty growl. 'You're driving me insane.'

'I'll take that as a compliment,' she said as another hot flush swept through her, 'but the way I see it any woman would suit your purpose. You don't strike me as the type to remain celibate for long. But don't expect me to satisfy your carnal desires because I won't do it.'

His hands fell from her shoulders and his mouth tightened. 'If that's really what you think then there's not much more I can say.'

She noticed that he didn't deny it. Besides, how could she get involved with a man whose attitude towards his son left a lot to be desired? Admittedly, he'd panicked when he had the kidnap threat, but prior to that he had put his work first, and probably would again. What sort of father was that?

If she ever married again—and it was a very big if— she would want a man who adored children, who would become the father Ben had never had. Andreas Papadakis certainly didn't fit the bill.

Peta went to bed, but not to sleep. She tried not to think of Andreas but that kiss insisted on resurrecting itself. She could feel his mouth on hers, feel the heat that rushed through every vein in her body, she even wriggled with excitement as though he were still touching her.

Damn the man! She had meant what she said. There would be no recurrences. She had to firmly fix it in her mind that he was her employer and she was to treat him as such—and that was the way she wanted him to treat her. But would he? Had she got through to him? Only time would tell.

CHAPTER SEVEN

ANDREAS threw himself into his work. His office in Athens was having staffing problems and he wanted to make some changes anyway. It was the perfect antidote. When finally he had thought he was getting his life back together Peta had declared she wanted nothing to do with him on a personal level.

He was finding it hard to handle. The woman drove him crazy. It would have been all right if he'd never kissed her—perhaps. If he hadn't felt the exciting heat of her body against his—maybe. If he hadn't been intoxicated by the sensual smell of her—possibly. But he had experienced all three, and there was no way that he was going to give up.

All he had to do was bide his time. She hadn't meant what she said, not deep down. It had been a heat-of-the-moment thing. He would show her. He would prove to her that she needed him as much as he needed her.

Neither of them wanted a permanent relationship. Peta didn't, she'd made that very clear, and he wasn't ready yet to put anyone into Maria's place. But why deny the extremely strong physical attraction they both felt? It could be termed as lust, he supposed, on his part anyway, but it felt something more than that. He didn't simply want to use her; she was too nice a person.

Even nice wasn't the right word to sum Peta up. It was a totally ineffective word. All he knew was that Peta entranced him.

But he showed her none of this. He'd decided that he would play it her way, for the time being.

Peta actually enjoyed giving lessons to the boys—except when Andreas's mother interrupted them. She seemed to think it was her given duty to supervise proceedings, and each day she would enter the playroom and silently watch. And as soon as she thought that Peta wasn't doing something correctly she would intervene.

'I'm no teacher,' flashed Peta on one occasion. 'I'm doing this because Andreas asked me to.'

'Andreas is a fool,' declared his mother. 'Quite easily I could employ a proper tutor.'

'Maybe Andreas thinks we won't be here that long.' Peta's blue eyes were hostile as she looked at the older woman. It was wishful thinking on her part, of course, she had no idea how long Andreas intended staying.

'He has said as much to you?' came the swift response.

Peta shrugged. 'Not in so many words.'

'Then I think it is you who does not want to stay. Believe me, my son is never happier than when he is with me here.'

Whether that was true or not Peta had no way of knowing. The fact that he *had* instinctively come here must mean something, though.

Most evenings when Andreas came home he was in a foul mood, and Peta kept well out of his way. Almost a week had passed since the kiss. A week in which she had relived it over and over again, had felt all the same sensations, but was still of the opinion that she had done the right thing.

On this particular evening, however, Andreas came home before she retired to her room. She'd just cleared away the toys the boys had used in the pool and was taking a moment to relax on the terrace when he rounded the corner of the house.

Her heart instantly stammered. He was wearing a lightweight business suit, the collar of his shirt undone, tie hanging loose. His eyes narrowed as he looked at her. 'Why have you been avoiding me?' he enquired sharply.

'What makes you think I have?' Peta's chin automatically rose in defence, and as she met the disturbing dark depths of his eyes she felt a slither of something suspiciously like desire. She had tried very hard to bury such feelings, had even thought she was succeeding, now she realised that they were still very much alive and in danger of giving her away.

'I haven't seen you for days.'

'That's your problem, not mine. I haven't left the house. If you're too busy to spend time with your son, don't take it out on me.' Now, why had she said that? It wasn't Nikos who was in question here. Although it was true he hardly ever saw the boy. He seemed content to leave him in her care.

'Let's leave Nikos out of this,' he rasped. 'It's you we're talking about. You hide away in your room as though you're afraid.'

Her eyes flashed a brilliant blue. 'I have no reason to be afraid, not of you.'

'That's right, no reason at all. So as soon as I've changed we're going out to dinner.'

Peta lifted her shoulders in a vague shrug. 'If that is your wish.'

'Be ready in half an hour.' And with a swift click of his heels he was gone.

Peta didn't move for a few seconds. She didn't want

to go out with him. She ought to have told him so, except that his tone had brooked no refusal. There had been a hardness in his eyes that she hadn't seen for a long time, so it definitely wasn't going to be a pleasurable evening.

Perhaps he wasn't happy with the way she was tutoring his son. His mother undoubtedly gave him running reports. Perhaps he was sending her back to England but softening the blow with an expensive meal. He didn't need her here, not when the child had a doting grandmother who gave him anything that he asked for.

She went up to her room and looked through her wardrobe. The fact that she owned only three summer dresses didn't make the decision hard. Mainly at home she wore tops and either skirts or trousers. Two of the dresses she'd originally bought for weddings; the third was a cornflower-blue sun-dress with shoelace-thin straps.

After showering she pulled on the blue dress and brushed her hair, twisting it up into a knot on the top of her head before applying the merest touch of mascara and lipstick. In less than half an hour she was back down.

'Good, you're ready. I hate a woman who keeps me waiting,' he announced crisply as she joined him on the terrace. 'Let's go.'

Andreas had changed into a pair of charcoal-grey trousers and a white linen shirt. His hair was still damp from the shower and he looked totally gorgeous. Peta hated to admit it but he did, and every sensitive point in her body absolutely refused to behave itself. It didn't augur well for the rest of the evening.

Sitting beside him in his car, even with the air-conditioning going full blast, she felt on fire. It had been a huge mistake agreeing to go out with him, except that he'd not given her much choice. Somehow she needed to control her errant emotions.

Their journey was made in silence. Stealing a glance at Andreas, Peta observed the grim set of his mouth and jaw, the way his long-fingered hands gripped the wheel so tightly that his knuckles shone white. Why he was so uptight she had no idea, and could only presume that she would soon find out.

The restaurant was a square white building almost in the middle of nowhere. Olive trees shaded it, a few distant houses offered some company, but there were no other cars parked outside. It didn't even look open.

She accompanied him inside and it took several long seconds for her eyes to become accustomed to the gloom. The windows were tiny and on every sill stood potted red geraniums, shutting out what little light there was. The tables had red gingham cloths and yet more geraniums in their centre.

Peta had been expecting something grander, and it must have reflected on her face because Andreas said, 'Don't judge by appearances. Mine host is a personal friend, the food is superb. In another hour or so there won't be an empty table in the place. There are tables out at the back or we can eat in here. Which would you prefer?'

'Indoors,' she said decisively. 'It's cooler.'

A short, stout, olive-skinned man emerged from a back room, and upon seeing Andreas he gave a shout of sheer pleasure. There was much back-slapping and hand-shaking and a volume of Greek. Finally the man turned to her, flashing a set of brilliant white teeth. 'And this is...?' he asked in broken English.

'Peta James,' introduced Andreas. 'Peta, this is Stellios, an old school-friend.'

Stellios made a great show of kissing her hand. 'You take her for your wife?'

Andreas shook his head. 'Peta looks after Nikos for me.'

'Ah, shame; she is very beautiful.' He clapped a hand to his heart. 'I marry you myself, except I already have wife.'

Peta dutifully laughed, though she felt somewhat embarrassed to be talked about like this.

'And Nikos?' went on the restaurant owner. 'You bring him to see me?'

'Soon,' promised Andreas. 'Soon.'

When the jovial man had gone they sat down and Peta picked up the menu. It was handwritten in Greek! She looked at it for perhaps half a minute, knowing she hadn't a cat in hell's chance of understanding it. 'I'll have what you have,' she said.

She looked up as she spoke and discovered to her dismay that Andreas was watching her. There was no expression on his face, nothing to tell her what he was thinking. His eyes were narrowed and calculating, and when they met hers it felt as though he had stabbed into her soul.

It was a swift, sharp pain and she almost winced because it felt so physical. And then it was gone. He dropped his gaze to the menu and she was left wondering what that look had meant.

'I think we'll let Stellios decide,' he said. 'What would you like to drink?'

'Water, please.'

'I can't tempt you with a glass of wine?'

Peta shook her head. And once the water had arrived,

and Stellios announced that he would bring to them a feast fit for a king, she asked the burning question. 'What am I doing here?'

There was the glimmer of a smile on his lips. 'You're having dinner with me, of course.'

'But why?'

'Because it doesn't look as though I'm going to see you any other way.'

'That's your fault; you're always out,' she declared hotly.

'There is much work to be done.'

Peta shook her head. 'Always work. Don't you ever stop to think that Nikos might want to spend some time with his father? You go out before he's up and come home after he's gone to bed.'

'Has he said anything?'

'Actually, no, but that's only because he has Ben to play with. You're failing in your duties, Mr Papadakis. I thought you were concerned about him.'

'I know he's safe here.'

'How do you know,' she argued, 'when you never see him?'

'My mother reports to me each evening.'

'I bet she does,' Peta flared. 'I bet she also tells you that I'm useless as a teacher. Exactly why have you brought me out here tonight? To give me my marching orders?'

A look of surprise crossed his face. 'Why would I want to do that?'

'Because I'm surplus to requirements. I don't fit in here, I never will.'

'You're talking nonsense, Peta. And as for your teaching abilities, I'll have a word with Nikos tomorrow, find out exactly what he has learned. My mother says you spend too long tutoring them; that is her only complaint.'

Peta wasn't sure that she believed him, and if she hadn't been hungry she would have suggested he take her home again. She didn't want this conversation. She didn't want to be sitting beside him in a little Greek restaurant where the owner kept popping his head round the door and smiling favourably on the two of them.

'Let's forget the whole thing,' said Andreas sharply. 'Let's concentrate on us.'

To what end? wondered Peta with a sharp stab of unease. 'What are you doing that's taking you away from the house for so many hours each day?' she asked, determined to steer the conversation away from anything personal.

One eyebrow lifted, as though he had guessed her tactics, nevertheless he answered evenly, 'I have an office in Athens—it's the main hub of my company. I'm restructuring it. If it wasn't for the fact that I need you to look after Nikos I'd whisk you away there to help me. Some of those girls don't know the first thing about efficiency.'

'I'm flattered,' she said. 'How long is this…restructuring going to take?'

'I have no idea.'

'So your son's going to see nothing of you for several more weeks?'

His lips tightened. 'You don't believe in pulling punches, do you?'

'I would never neglect Ben.'

'Nikos isn't neglected,' he declared harshly. 'Don't say that. I love my son dearly.'

'Do you ever tell him? Do you ever show it? Dammit, Andreas, kids aren't kids for long. He'll be grown up before you know it and then you'll wish that you'd spent more time with him.'

His eyes became glacial. 'I didn't bring you out to discuss my son,' he snarled, clearly resenting the home truths.

Peta raised her finely shaped brows. 'So—if it's not to sack me, and it's not because of Nikos, that leaves only one thing. But it won't work, Andreas. I'm not interested in you, not now, not ever.'

He looked at her long and hard, searing her skin with an uncomfortable heat. 'You're an attractive woman, Peta. I find it hard to believe that you won't let a man into your life. Have you had any boyfriends since Ben's father let you down?'

'Not that it's any of your business, but, yes, there have been a couple,' she admitted reluctantly.

'And?'

'And nothing. They didn't work out,' she retorted.

'Because you presented the ice-maiden image, the same as you're trying to do now.'

'Trying has nothing to do with it,' she flashed. 'It's how I feel. I've never yet met a man I can trust.'

She watched as Andreas sucked in a deep breath, straightening his spine, his brown eyes coldly penetrating hers. She had insulted his manhood, but it was true. She would dearly love to meet a man whom she could love deeply and who would never let her down. Andreas wasn't that man. Andreas was still in love with Maria. He wanted her for her body alone and that she could do without.

'How do you know whether or not you can trust a man unless you relax your rigid attitude?' And still those stony brown eyes held hers.

Little did he know it but there had been many times

when she'd been prepared to relax where he was concerned; times when she had indeed let down her guard and almost given in to the clamouring needs of her body. But that wasn't the way to go. And she would be as well to remember it.

'I think when the right man comes along I will know,' she told him bravely, and she was saved from having to elaborate further by their first course arriving in the form of several plates heaped with various appetisers. Some she recognised; some she didn't—baby squid, whitebait, stuffed vine leaves, salads with feta cheese, fresh crusty bread, various dips...so much that it was confusing.

'We'll never get through this lot!' she exclaimed. It was enough to fill her up without the main course.

'Just eat what you fancy,' he said with a wry smile. 'A little of each, perhaps? We can save the salad for later if it's too much.'

Everything was tasty and succulent and Peta tucked in with an appetite she hadn't expected. She drank her water, and when Andreas ordered a carafe of wine she obligingly sipped from her glass. She'd be careful, though, she told herself; she'd drink only enough to help her get through the evening.

Not that it was proving too much of an ordeal. Their conversation had turned to ordinary everyday things and this she could handle. As the evening progressed she could feel herself mellowing, and she even laughed out loud at some of Andreas's anecdotes.

Andreas too had relaxed in his attitude towards her. He was no longer cold and condemning but warm and welcoming. In fact the whole evening was turning into a much more pleasant affair than she'd expected.

'You have a beautiful smile, do you know that?' he asked suddenly.

Peta stopped smiling.

So did Andreas. 'For heaven's sake, Peta, I'm not try-ing to come on to you. I've already learned that that was a huge mistake.'

'I'm sorry,' she said instantly.

'You're just so used to closing up when a man pays you compliments.'

'I guess so.'

'Then stop it.' He reached out and put his hand over hers where it rested on the table.

Peta felt an incredible heat run through her and she prayed silently that he couldn't feel it, too. This was stupid. He was offering the hand of friendship, nothing more, why couldn't she take it? She'd always used the excuse that it was because Joe had stuffed up on her, but it now occurred to her that it had nothing to do with Joe and everything to do with herself.

She was happy living alone with her son, she didn't want a man in her life—and who was she trying to kid? Andreas was everything she had ever wanted in a man. He was handsome, he was exciting, he was sexy, and once she'd got through the hard tycoon image she had found out that he could be charming and attentive. He would make a good father if he didn't work so hard. Nikos adored him, didn't seem to resent the fact that he didn't see much of him. He was a well-adjusted child who was obviously used to this kind of lifestyle.

But getting too close to Andreas would be like living with a time bomb. It was wrong to be jealous of Maria but Peta was. Andreas didn't talk about her, and it was this fact that was the problem. His mother said he still loved her, and for some reason Peta couldn't even ex-plain to herself she believed the woman.

A *ménage à trois* wouldn't work. He would pay her

attention, he would flatter her, he would take her body and use her—and she like a fool would let him—but he would offer her nothing at the end of it all. His heart was too deeply entrenched in the mother of his child.

All of these thoughts flashed through her mind as his hand held hers and she would have dearly loved to snatch it away, but that would only confirm what he had just said. So she let it lie there, she let the heat course through veins and arteries, she let her pulses and heart-beat quicken, and an incredible need stole over her.

Whether her features softened, whether something happened to alert Andreas to the way she felt, Peta didn't know, but his eyes darkened as though he had picked up on an unspoken message and, lifting her hand to his mouth, he kissed it.

He kissed the back first, trailing feather-light kisses all over, and then her fingers, each one separately, until finally he turned her hand and pressed a kiss into her palm before curling her fingers over it. It was as though he was saying, Hold that kiss. Keep it and think of me.

Unable to help herself, she looked deeply into his eyes, saw a need that reflected her own, held that gaze, and was stupidly disappointed when he was the first to look away.

'More wine?' he asked pleasantly.

Peta shook her head. 'No, thanks.' She hadn't even finished the glass he'd poured her and she didn't intend to. There were going to be no repeats of that fateful night when she'd conceived Ben.

During the rest of the meal, between visits by the attentive, always smiling Stellios—who, she was sure, had already in his own mind got them married—their conversation skirted around everything except the way they felt. But it was there nevertheless, hovering over them like a bad smell, making sure its presence never went away.

The room had filled but neither of them was aware of it, not until Andreas suggested they leave and she looked around. What had happened to her? How had she become so immersed in Andreas that she'd been oblivious to what was going on around her?

He paid the bill and they went out to the car, to a jewelled sky and a crescent moon that promised a new beginning. He opened her door but before she could slide in she found herself enveloped in arms so strong they almost hurt.

'I can't do this,' he growled. 'I can't ignore you. You're driving me crazy, woman, do you know that?' His mouth claimed hers with a suddenness that allowed no retreat. 'I want you; I need you, you have to let me in, Peta. Forget that bastard who screwed you up; let me show you that there's more to life than you're currently experiencing.'

He had been driving her crazy all evening, too. She hadn't been looking forward to crawling into bed without her needs satisfied. So when his mouth swooped on hers Peta made no attempt to stop him.

The kiss sent her senses spinning into orbit and without even a second thought she parted her lips. He seemed to pause, to wonder at her change of heart, and then with a groan his tongue plunged deep inside. He tasted, he explored, he tormented. Peta whimpered.

This was heaven; this was the stuff of dreams. A tall, dark, handsome stranger sweeping her off her feet. Except that he wasn't a stranger, he was her boss. But it made no difference. She wanted him, he wanted her; it was simple.

There was nothing simple about the kiss, though. It

didn't stop at a kiss for long. His hands touched and stroked, sometimes gently, evoking the sweetest, headiest response, sometimes hard and purposeful, pressing her to him so that she couldn't help but feel his throbbing arousal.

Her excitement increased and her arms snaked around him without her being aware of it. She was suddenly full of desperate hunger, didn't care that at the end of the day it would be goodbye and thanks. This was now, this was her deepest desires being satisfied. This was something she had never before experienced, not with this intensity, not with this ferocity.

'This isn't the right place,' he declared gruffly as another car full of diners pulled up, headlights catching their embrace full-beam. 'Let's go home.'

During the drive Peta couldn't help but wonder whether she was doing the right thing. Was this something she would regret come morning? Or was this the beginning of a new and wonderful relationship? He excited her so much, this man. Sitting close to him now kept her senses inflamed, helped by the way he kept darting warm, intimate glances at her, by the way his hand reached across and touched her thigh or her hand.

When they reached the house he moved around the car to open her door, reaching down to help her out, crushing her against him, sending another mindless storm of sensation and need chasing wantonly through her body. But for only a brief moment.

She'd had time to reflect, to decide that this wasn't the way she wanted things to go. It was too soon; he was rushing her. One day, maybe, perhaps in the not too distant future even. But first she needed to come to terms with the new feelings her body was experiencing.

'What's wrong?' he asked as she pulled away from him.

'I can't do this, not yet.'

'Lord,' he exploded. 'I thought you'd got over that. Earlier you—'

'I was intoxicated by the wine and the food and the general ambience. I let myself get carried away,' she answered swiftly. 'But it's not what I want.'

One eyebrow rose. 'No? I think you're kidding yourself, lady. I think you want it very much indeed. Some mistaken sense of reproach for what you did nine years ago is blinding your judgement.'

'Maybe you're right,' she admitted, seizing the excuse. 'But I can't help it.' Adding as they walked into the house, 'I'm going to my room. Alone.'

At that precise moment his mother called out. 'Is that you, Andreas? I'd like a word.'

He swore beneath his breath. 'Your reprieve,' he snarled.

But for how long? she wondered. Andreas wasn't known for his patience. She'd given herself away, shown him that she wasn't exactly resistant to his advances. There'd be no peace now.

And she didn't have to wait long. She'd just come out of the shower and was wearing nothing more than a towel, when, with a mere cursory knock, he burst into her room.

CHAPTER EIGHT

'GET out!' shot a startled Peta. 'Didn't I make myself clear, Andreas? I'm not yet ready to start up a relationship with you. And I certainly don't intend to—'

'Shut up,' he instructed. 'This isn't about you and me, it's about Nikos.'

Peta's hands shot to her mouth. What had happened? She ought never to have gone out and left the boys. Why had she let Andreas persuade her? Why had she put pleasure before duty? Pleasure with a capital P as well, because that was certainly what the kiss had been all about.

Looking at him more closely, she could see that all hunger and desire had gone from his face. It was strained now and pale; she ought to have noticed straight away. Something tragic had happened, and it was all her fault.

'Tell me,' she said quickly.

'The would-be kidnapper—or kidnappers, whatever the case may be—has traced us here.'

'What?' She almost screamed the word and her heart beat a rapid tattoo within her breast. The towel slipped and she strove frantically to save it but failed. Not that Andreas seemed to notice her nakedness. His eyes didn't even flicker. She re-wrapped the towel, tucking the end in firmly, but holding it as well just in case.

'Another threatening letter's arrived,' he informed her. 'My mother's furious that I didn't tell her the real reason we were here.'

'We could move the boys' beds into my room if that would help,' she suggested. 'There's plenty of space.

117

And you can rest assured I'll keep my eye on Nikos every second of the day.'

'No need,' he said, shaking his head brusquely. 'We're leaving.'

'Again?' she queried, her eyes wide with shock. 'You can't keep running, Andreas, you have to do something. These people must be caught. Have you informed the police?' It didn't seem long since she'd asked him the same question, and yet it must be all of three weeks. Three weeks it had taken whoever it was to find them. Not long. There would be no escape. Wherever they ended up they would be found. Her heart felt as heavy as lead.

'The police suggested it,' he told her shortly. 'At least they're taking this whole thing a lot more seriously than they did in England. Unfortunately they don't have sufficient manpower to protect us while they investigate. So—I'm going to take you and the boys to a mountain hideaway tonight under cover of darkness. We won't be found there.'

An icy shiver raced down Peta's spine. She didn't like the sound of this one little bit. But Andreas wasn't a man you could argue with, especially in this mood.

'If it was myself in danger,' he added, 'I'd stay and face whoever it is that's doing this to me. But where Nikos is concerned I cannot take the risk. So get packing,' he ordered brusquely. 'I'll wake the boys.'

He left the room as quickly as he'd entered. Peta threw on some clothes and heaved out a suitcase. In less than half an hour they were on their way.

Andreas was grim-faced as he drove, and they'd been going well over an hour and a half before he headed up into the blackness of the mountains. The boys had fallen asleep again but he didn't speak, and Peta didn't dare ask any questions.

Eventually they left the mountain road, following what felt like a bumpy cart track going nowhere, and after much twisting and turning the Range Rover's headlights picked out a small stone cabin tucked well into the trees.

'This is it,' he announced tersely. 'Boys, wake up, we're here.'

Ben and Nikos helped carry everything in while Andreas got the generator going. They loved the thought of charging around in the middle of the night, especially when they discovered that they were going to share a bedroom. The trouble was there were only two bedrooms, tiny rooms with a double bed in each, and a dresser and a wardrobe, and not much room to walk around.

Peta looked doubtfully at the second bedroom as she began to unpack the few clothes she'd brought with her. Of one thing she was sure; she wasn't sharing a bed with Andreas Papadakis.

As well as the bedrooms there was a kitchen, a living room and a bathroom. The same amount of space that she'd had at home for herself and Ben, and now there were four of them!

The boys went eagerly to bed and at last she was alone with Andreas. 'We'll be safe now,' he said confidently as they sat down in the tiny living room.

'But for how long?' she wanted to know. 'We can't stay here for ever.'

'Of course not,' he assured her. 'But, whatever you do, don't alarm the boys.'

'What excuse did you give them for leaving at such an ungodly hour?'

He grinned then, his teeth flashing white. 'I told them it was a huge adventure and I had lots of surprises for them. Believe me, they'll love it.'

'It doesn't feel like an adventure to me,' Peta declared sharply. 'For one thing I'm worried stiff, and for another I want to know what the sleeping arrangements are when there's only one bed between the two of us.'

His lips twisted wryly and there was an amazing twinkle in his eye. 'I wondered when you'd get around to that.'

'As a matter of fact, forget I asked,' she retorted quickly. 'I'll take the bed, you can sleep where the hell you like.' She looked doubtfully at the couch on which he was sitting. It didn't look long enough to accommodate a man who was well over six feet, but why should she care? 'Whose cabin is this, anyway?'

'It's mine—my mountain retreat,' he answered. 'Some of my friends use it but it's where I come when things get on top of me.'

Peta lifted her brows. 'How often is that?' She somehow couldn't see anything getting on top of Andreas. He was the most together person she'd ever met. He was perfectly in control of his life—and those around him! It was only now, when his son was in danger, that she'd seen him lose it a little. But not much. He'd quickly worked out a plan of action and put it into operation.

'There have been times,' he admitted, a shadow she was beginning to recognise darkening his eyes.

Like when his wife had died, she quickly surmised. She should have thought of that. 'Has Nikos been here before?'

'No. It's just as much an experience for him as it is for Ben. You'll see, Peta, they'll have the time of their lives.'

'Is there a phone?' What if the kidnapper traced them here? What if the boys fell and seriously hurt themselves?

'No, and my mobile doesn't work up here either. It's what I like best about it.'

The man who was always in touch, always on the phone, always planning and organising, actually liked being cut off?

'You look as though you find it hard to believe.'

'I do,' she said at once. 'You thrive on work; you're never away from it. You'll be bored silly in a couple of days.'

'With two lively youngsters? To say nothing of a very beautiful young woman?' His eyes held hers as he spoke.

Warning bells rang. Peta shook her head. 'I'm here for Nikos's sake, not yours.'

He held up his hands, palms facing her. 'Did I say anything different?'

He was making it sound as though she was the one jumping to conclusions. Peta's blue eyes flashed across the room. 'It's not what you said but the way that you said it.'

'And you're suggesting that I keep well away from you? Not so much as a tiny goodnight kiss? You're going to force me to sleep on this tiny couch while you lie there in my bed and think about me.'

'As if!' A flare of indignant light blazed in Peta's eyes.

'Oh, I think you will,' he said. 'I don't think you'll be able to help yourself, even if it's only to feel guilty.'

'Never!'

His lips quirked. He didn't believe her.

Well, she would show him. She jumped to her feet.

'As a matter of fact I'm going to bed now. Goodnight, Mr Papadakis.'

His eyes narrowed at the formality. 'Sleep tight, Miss James.'

'I will, don't worry.'

She'd just got undressed and into bed, when the door opened.

'Pardon me for intruding,' Andreas said with exaggerated politeness as he snapped on the light, 'but I believe my holdall is in here.'

Her wide blue eyes watched warily as he moved into the room. 'I don't think so,' she snapped, knowing that he was using it as an excuse. 'I'd have seen it if it was.'

'I also need a couple of sheets and a pillow.'

He found what he wanted on a high shelf in the wardrobe, his holdall had been tossed in there, too. Peta's lips thinned. He'd intended sleeping in here all along—until she'd put her foot down. But she didn't care. There was no way he was sharing her bed, even if he did manage to arouse every one of her baser instincts.

Beneath the sheets her body was ready to go up in flames. All her senses had gone into overdrive, and she was so aware of him that she felt sure he must know it. She tried closing her eyes but that was worse, because she didn't know then what he was doing.

Please hurry up and go, she prayed silently. But he seemed in no hurry. He put the holdall down while he slowly and carefully folded the sheets over his arm.

'If you're waiting for an invitation to join me it will be a long night,' she thrust acidly.

'Why are you denying what you really want?' It was a sexual growl, narrowed eyes fixed intently on hers.

It sent a further tingle through her limbs. 'I want more

than anything to be left alone to get some sleep,' she
declared shakily. 'I thought it was all sorted.'

'You'd condemn me to that hard, lumpy couch?'

'It didn't look hard and lumpy to me,' she riposted.
Goodness, when was he going to get the message? Because the truth was the longer he stood there looking at
her, the weaker she was becoming.

'And not even a mite small?'

'So what?' she demanded. 'It was your idea that we
come here.'

'Not my idea that we sleep in separate rooms.'

'Then you should have thought about it before we left.
You should have known I wouldn't even dream about
sleeping with you.'

'Is that so?' Lazy, mocking eyes laughed into hers. 'I
think the lady lies. I think you've thought about it a lot.
In fact I think you even like the idea.' As he spoke he
walked around the foot of the bed to her side.

'No, I don't,' she claimed, shocked to hear how husky
her voice sounded.

'OK, if the lady says no then the lady means no. But
a goodnight kiss will do no harm, will it?'

Andreas saw the panic in Peta's eyes as he bent over
her, and for a brief second wondered whether he ought
to back off. But, no, faint heart never won fair lady—
wasn't that what they said? And he was certainly not
known for being faint-hearted.

She smelled so sweet, looked so lovely, that his male
hormones wouldn't behave themselves. And as his lips
lightly brushed hers he felt a tremor run through her.
Nor was it a tremor of fear; it was desire, he was certain
of it. She wasn't as immune as she made out; he'd
proved that before when he'd kissed her. No matter how

much she protested Peta James was one hell of a sexy lady. An aroused sexy lady!

He'd intended the kiss to be light and friendly, so what was happening to him? Why was he deepening it? Why was he taking the chance of spoiling everything? Because he couldn't help himself, that was why. He wanted to jump into bed with her right now; he wanted to take her into his arms; he wanted to make love to her; he wanted everything!

But he couldn't do that because it would ruin the time they had to spend here. He must never forget that Nikos's safety was his first priority. And he needed Peta to help look after his son. He mustn't antagonise her.

So he raised his head. It took an achingly long time to do so. He felt as though he was held to her by a magnet, and the pull was so strong that it took an enormous effort to break the bond.

He expected a further flow of indignation and anger, was surprised and somewhat pleased when all she did was turn away, letting the back of her head speak for itself. Disapproval, yes, but also an unhappiness within herself for allowing him to kiss her.

He smiled softly as he left the room. It was certainly a step in the right direction.

The couch was as hard and uncomfortable as he had known it would be. It wasn't made for tall men to sleep on—not for anyone to sleep on. Only once before had he attempted to sleep there. The roof had developed a leak during the winter and heavy rain had ruined both beds. He'd hardly slept a wink, and the very next day he'd had the roof fixed and new beds delivered. He'd sworn that he'd never sleep on that couch again.

Until a little minx by the name of Peta James had forced him to do so. He could, of course, have sent Ben in to sleep with his mother while he climbed in beside Nikos, but that would have created a precedent and spoilt any chance he had of ever sharing a bed with the woman who was beginning to drive him insane.

He had thought never to love again after Maria died, had thought it would be disloyal to her memory, especially as he blamed himself, and he wasn't even sure that he was in love now. All he did know was that this very beautiful redhead had got beneath his skin. He wanted her so badly that he was prepared to go to almost any lengths to persuade her into his bed.

When dawn began to streak the purple sky he climbed stiffly from the couch and, picking up a towel, quietly made his way outside. A hundred yards or so higher up the mountain was a natural rock pool deep enough to bathe in. It was a favourite spot of his, always guaranteed to soothe the mind as well as the body.

The chill of the water took his breath away but it did nothing to cool the rampant feelings he had where Peta was concerned. He came out of the pool feeling as hungry for her body as he had when he went in. He was finding it impossible to dismiss the thought of her.

Perhaps it had been a bad idea to bring her up here with him. Maybe he should have come with Nikos alone. Maybe he should never have brought her to Greece in the first place.

Suddenly he sensed that he was being watched and his first thoughts were of the kidnapper.

And he had left the boys alone with a sleeping Peta! Some protection she would be!

Heavens, he had allowed himself to be sidetracked by a pretty woman, forgetting the real reason he was here. He spun around—and in the half-light caught sight of a moving shadowy shape through the trees. Someone was keeping an eye on him while his accomplice did the dirty work!

With a yell, and heedless of the fact that he hadn't a stitch on, he sprinted in the direction of the shape, took a flying leap and landed on top of him. Except that it wasn't a he. 'Peta!' he exclaimed as the awfulness of the situation hit him. 'What the devil are you doing here?'

Peta had thought herself unobserved, had been unprepared when Andreas came charging in her direction, and was now both embarrassed and breathless as he got to his feet and glared down at her. She could hardly avoid looking at him, and at close quarters he was even more magnificent than he had been a dozen yards away. His immediately rampant manhood sent a rapid response through her limbs.

She scrambled with feverish haste to her feet so that at least her eyes could meet his on a level without other things coming between them. 'I—I heard you leave. I wondered where you were going. I—'

'Dammit, I could have killed you, skulking in the undergrowth like that. I thought you were one of the kidnappers. You had no right leaving the boys alone.'

'You said they wouldn't find us here.' She rubbed her shoulder where she had fallen. Already it was beginning to ache.

'You'd better get back to them,' he snarled. 'And if you want to see my naked body all you have to do is ask.' He turned his back on her and tramped to the pool, where he snatched up the towel and wrapped it tightly around his loins.

Peta found it impossible to move. He had the most gorgeous olive-skinned body. Lean hips, muscular shoulders and arms, but not overtly so; whorls of dark chest hair arrowing downwards, disappearing beneath the white towel. She'd been unable to take her eyes off him, had even been tempted to join him in the pool.

Simply looking at him had stirred her senses, sent the blood scorching through her veins. Want and need had taken over and she'd been on the point of making her presence known when he'd spotted her. She hadn't even had time to anticipate his action before he'd sent her crashing to the floor.

'I thought I told you to get back to the boys.' Andreas's eyes were glacially hard, his whole body tense with rejection. 'If Nikos has come to any harm then you'd better look out.'

Peta snapped back to life, but too late; he was already striding down the mountain. She followed more slowly, conscious that she had neglected her duty and he had every right to be angry, but confident that nothing would have happened to the boys.

For most of the night she had tossed and turned, thinking about Andreas, wondering how he was coping on the couch, almost giving in and suggesting they swap places. She had heard him get up and leave. What had made her decide to follow she didn't know, but she had checked Ben and Nikos first and they were both fast asleep.

If she hadn't been so fascinated by his naked body she would have made her presence known, but one look and she'd been hooked, and the longer she'd stood there the harder it had become to call out. It had triggered so many responses that she'd felt as if she was melting on the spot.

As she'd expected, the boys were still asleep, but Andreas didn't apologise. Instead, after pulling on a pair of shorts, he jumped into the Range Rover. 'I'm going to fetch supplies,' he announced. 'What little I brought won't last long. And I'm warning you, don't leave Nikos alone, not for one second.'

Her eyes widened. 'Don't you think you're overreacting?'

'You'd feel the same if it was Ben,' he told her coldly.

'So what was the point in coming up here if you're going to be paranoid? Nikos is an intelligent boy; he's sure to pick up on it.'

He started the engine. 'What I do is my business and you'd do as well to remember that.'

In other words she was here to do as he asked, not to question it. She heaved a sigh as he disappeared down the mountain. Some adventure this was proving to be. His anger was because she'd had the temerity to stare at his naked body, nothing else; not fear for Nikos. Well, he needn't worry, she wouldn't look at him again.

While waiting for the boys to wake she spent her time cleaning the cabin. It was a fairly impersonal place with not much in the way of ornaments or pictures. The uneven stone walls had once been painted white but were now a dingy grey. It needed sprucing up, she felt, although if it was used so infrequently was it worth it? She couldn't see Andreas feeling the need to escape very often.

In the bedroom she finished putting away her things, hanging Andreas's stuff in the wardrobe, too. It was in one of the drawers that she found the snapshot. Peta stared at it for a long time. Maria was beautiful; there was no getting away from it. Even more beautiful here than she was in the portrait done in oils. Rich raven-black hair, sensual lips and wide-spaced almond-shaped eyes. And so like Nikos that it was no wonder Andreas was reminded of his wife every time he looked at him. There was no way she could compete with a woman like this, with her extraordinary beauty and such a wealth of love for the man behind the camera radiating from her eyes.

The sound of voices had her spinning around. 'Mum, we're hungry.'

The spell was broken. And in half an hour Andreas returned.

They spent most of the day wandering through the forest, the children playing hide-and-seek, splashing beneath waterfalls, finding all sorts of natural treasures which they stuffed into their pockets for looking at again later.

Peta deliberately kept all conversation between herself and Andreas impersonal, which wasn't hard when he virtually ignored her. What was hard was ignoring the messages her body kept relaying. It was impossible to stand close and not be aware of him. Impossible to control the quivering sensations he created inside her.

When night-time came she insisted that he take the bed and she the couch.

'If that is your wish,' he said with pained politeness. 'But don't put yourself out on my behalf.'

'I think it will be best,' she answered.

He made no further objections.

As Peta lay there, curled up in the foetal position, she couldn't help thinking how uncomfortable he must have been. It was no wonder he'd got up at the crack of dawn. Amazingly, though, probably because they'd spent the day in the fresh air, she didn't have any trouble dropping off to sleep.

It didn't please her when she got up the following morning to discover that Andreas had beaten her to it and already gone out, because it meant that he'd had to walk past her, might even have stood looking down at her. Her cheeks grew hot at the thought. Her nightie had ended up as usual around her waist, and although the cover had been pulled over her when she awoke, how was she to know that it hadn't slipped off during the night and Andreas had replaced it?

Where was he? At the pool again? She longed to go and look but knew that she dared not. It didn't stop her imagination running riot, though. It was so easy to picture his hard naked body. He'd been perfectly at ease with it, no inhibitions whatsoever, even when he stood right in front of her. Whereas she, Lord help her, had been whipped by a frenzy of unwanted emotions.

If he'd taken her into his arms at that moment she'd have let him undress her, let him lay her on the ground and make love to her. Even the thought of it sent a wild yearning through her body. She shook her head. *Stop this, Peta,* she warned herself. *Stop it this instant. This man is not for you.*

The shower in the cabin was erratic, to say the least, and as she stood beneath it Peta thought longingly of the natural pool. If only she'd woken before Andreas she could have gone up there herself. Tomorrow, she promised herself. Tomorrow she would do it.

The boys had already eaten their breakfast by the time Andreas returned. He looked hot and his hair was dry, so he'd obviously either not bathed or been out of the pool for some time.

'Where have you been?' Nikos posed the question Peta was dying to ask.

Andreas grinned. 'I thought we'd have a treasure hunt today, if that's all right with you boys? I've been setting it up.'

They both jumped up and down and said yes in unison.

'That's settled, then, but I need my breakfast first.'

Peta thought how much younger he looked when he smiled, and how much more relaxed he was with the boys than he was with her. 'We've had toast and cereal,' she said, 'but if you'd like an omelette I can easily—'

'Toast and cereal will do fine for me, too,' he said easily. 'Nikos, I think you'd better put some sturdier shoes on; you, too, Ben.'

As the boys ran off to do his bidding Andreas followed Peta into the kitchen. 'How was the couch?' he asked casually as she placed cereal boxes on the table and filled a jug with milk.

'I slept OK,' she admitted.

'You looked more comfortable than I felt on it.'

'Are you suggesting that I take the couch every night?' she asked sharply as she sliced bread and placed it beneath the grill. 'Because that wasn't my idea when I offered to change places. I think maybe we should do it turn and turn about.'

'And I think maybe if you stopped being so prickly we could share the bed.'

Peta's back was turned to Andreas as he spoke and she unconsciously stiffened, not turning to face him for several long seconds. 'I can't believe you've said that.'

His lips turned down at the corners and his shoulders lifted slightly. 'It seems a perfectly logical decision.'

'Logical, maybe,' she returned huffily, 'but sensible, no. I can't imagine anything worse than sharing a bed with a man who means nothing to me.' Except that he had the ability to set every one of her nerve-ends quivering whenever he was near. Sleeping with him would prove impossible. Sleep she wouldn't. Ignite she most definitely would.

'It's funny,' he said as he sat down at the table and tipped cornflakes into a bowl. 'My impression is very different. I think I do mean something to you, but I also think that you're scared to admit it.'

'Scared?' she echoed. 'Why should I be scared? I'm my own woman. I have full control of my life.' Hell, what a stupid thing to say. She didn't have control of it at all, he did. He'd had it ever since she'd begun to work for him. She'd used to be in control, yes, but not any longer. Everything he'd asked her to do she'd done, even so far as coming here with him. But she was definitely drawing the line at sharing a bed. All he wanted her for was to satisfy his male hunger, and that she could do without.

'If you have control, why do you fall to pieces whenever I look at you in a certain way? Why do you respond to my kisses?'

'Because you're one hell of a sexy man, that's why,' she flared. 'You might not have been aware of it but every woman in the company used to swoon at the mere sight of you.'

Eyebrows rose. 'Did you?'

'Actually, no,' she admitted. 'And because you stir my senses now it doesn't mean that I want to hop into bed with you. Maybe it's because I was once bitten. I don't know. All I do know is that I'm not prepared to let you use my body.'

Her choice of words had him scowling. 'I don't think I've ever been guilty of using a woman for personal gratification. It's always been a two-way thing.'

'Have there been women since Maria?' she dared to ask.

'Yes.'

'And are you telling me that you didn't use them?'

'I had needs,' he admitted, 'but so did they. And so do you,' he added, his voice deepening to a sensual growl.

Just the way he said it caused the pulse at the base of her throat to flutter. 'But my needs are obviously not as great as yours.'

'I think you've burnt the toast.'

Peta swung around quickly. Smoke was rising from the grill. 'Damn!' she exclaimed, adding a few more choice swear words beneath her breath. 'It's your fault.' She tipped the toast smartly into the bin, but when she reached out for the loaf to cut two more slices he stopped her.

'Don't bother. I'm not that hungry anyway.'

Peta began to cough.

'You'd better get out,' he said, flapping a tea towel to try and get rid of the smoke. 'See if the boys are ready. I'll finish up in here.'

She was glad to go, because not only had the toast nearly set on fire, but she was also on fire. All this talk about sleeping together had set off a chain reaction, and each nerve and vein and pulse that it touched jumped louder than the others until her whole body was jangling.

The boys were outside, raring to go, and she drew in much-needed breaths of fresh mountain air. Not that it did a lot of good. It would take more than air to rid her mind and body of Andreas Papadakis. And the longer they were forced together the harder it was going to be.

When Andreas was ready he handed out the first clue, and after studying it for a few minutes Ben and Nikos ran off, laughing. Peta followed more leisurely, conscious of Andreas a few yards away, his eyes ever-watchful on the boys. And probably on herself, too, though she tried not to think of it.

A quarter of an hour passed, and they had all found the second clue and worked it out when Andreas fell into step at her side. 'The boys are enjoying themselves.'

'Yes, indeed,' she agreed. 'It was a good idea of yours.'

'Perhaps now we can finish our conversation.'

Peta frowned as she quickly looked at him. 'What are you talking about?'

'Needs. The fact that you said mine was greater than yours. I don't agree.'

'Not when you're the one who's pushing for an affair?' she asked scornfully.

'Not an affair. You make it sound sordid.'

'So what is it you want?' she demanded. 'You know as well as I do that you're still in love with your wife. No one will ever be able to take her place. What would you do if I let you make love to me? Pretend that I was Maria?'

Oh, Lord, she shouldn't have said that. It was cruel and unasked-for. And when she saw the hurt in his eyes and the angry black shadow across his face she clapped her hands to her mouth. 'I'm sorry,' she said quietly. 'So sorry.'

CHAPTER NINE

ANDREAS walked away from Peta. Her careless words hurt, deeply. If that was the impression he gave then he was doing something wrong. It was true, no one would ever take Maria's place; she would always be very special in his heart. But Peta was different in every way, surely she knew that? He wanted her for herself alone, not as a replacement for Maria.

He strode after the boys; they were having a whale of a time, laughing and running, arguing light-heartedly over the clue, eventually finding the ancient olive tree with the clue tucked into one of its lower branches.

He had thought today would be fun for all of them, had never expected Peta to say something so hurtful. Admittedly she had immediately apologised, but it was the fact that she even thought he would do something like that. If he made love to Peta he certainly wouldn't be thinking about Maria. The two women were as different as chalk from cheese.

'Steady, boys,' he said as they came hurtling back down towards him.

'This is fun,' said Nikos. 'Where's Peta? Why isn't she joining in?'

Andreas turned and was surprised to see that she was nowhere in sight. Surely she hadn't gone back to the house? But he dared not go looking and leave the boys. Although he felt reasonably confident that whoever was threatening to kidnap his son wouldn't trace them up here, he wasn't prepared to take the risk.

'I guess she's still searching for the clue,' he said.

Ben laughed. 'Mummy's not as clever as us, is she?' And he ran off again.

Peta didn't know how she could have been so thoughtless. Andreas felt bad enough about losing his wife without her slamming into him like that. She'd been guilty of thinking of herself alone.

She'd sat down on a boulder when Andreas walked off, burying her head in her hands, wondering how she could rectify the situation. All she could do was apologise again, but the truth was no amount of apology would set the matter right. She'd been completely out of order.

'Mummy, what's the matter?'

Peta looked up as Ben came running towards her, Nikos not far behind.

'I have a headache,' she lied, thinking quickly.

'Does that mean we have to go back?'

'Of course not, darling,' she said, shaking her head. 'All I needed was a few moments to myself. How are you doing?'

'We've found two clues,' he answered importantly, his little chest swelling with pride. 'Will you be all right if we carry on?'

'Of course your mother will be all right.' Andreas spoke over her son's shoulder. 'I'll look after her.'

Peta's mouth twisted wistfully. She'd give anything to be able to retract those thoughtlessly spoken words. There was still pain in Andreas's deep brown eyes, but, thank goodness, he didn't look as though he was going to hold it against her.

'What can I say?' she asked, looking up at him sorrowfully as the boys ran away.

'I think it's best forgotten. Let's follow.'

They chatted as the boys raced around, and on the surface they were friends again, but the intimacy was lost. There were no more suggestions on his part that they share a bed. No innuendoes, no soft, hungry glances. It was gone. Dashed away by a few words.

She ought to be pleased, but she wasn't. Contrarily, she wanted him, wanted to share closeness with him because he excited her. He had awoken long-dead feelings. He had made her feel all woman again. No man had done that in a long time.

Ought she to apologise once more? But one look at his face told her it would do no good. There was a sternness to the beetling brows, a tightness to his mouth, and although when he spoke to her he sounded perfectly normal Peta knew that inside he was hurting like hell.

And she didn't blame him. What she had said was unforgivable.

The boys found the treasure—a carved wooden boat they could play with in the bathing pool—and they all made their way home.

For the rest of the day Andreas played with the boys and Peta busied herself around the little house.

'I think it will be best if you take the bed,' said Andreas later that evening when the boys were asleep and they were sitting outside, enjoying the stillness.

'Why?' she wanted to know. She didn't deserve the bed. 'It's not fair on you. I'll sleep on the couch. I can quite easily manage there.'

'I said, you take the bed,' he answered tersely. 'There's nothing more to be said.'

Peta couldn't understand. If she had to sleep on the couch for the rest of their stay it would be what she deserved. Why wasn't he punishing her? Why was he punishing himself?

'Just for tonight, then,' she agreed.

'Every night, dammit!' he shot back. 'Just do as you're told.'

'But—'

'But nothing.' Stony brown eyes fixed unrelentingly on hers. 'Go to bed, Peta. Go now!'

It was a long and lonely night. Peta tossed and turned, unable to stop thinking about Andreas, wondering whether he was managing to sleep, how comfortable he was. If it hadn't been for her crass insensitivity they might well have been sleeping together.

Her heart pounded at the very thought. But it was one best not delved into. It would never happen, not now. She had well and truly put a stop to any romantic developments.

During the next few days Andreas was friendly enough on the surface. Ben and Nikos never suspected that anything was wrong, but for some unknown reason the fact that he showed not the remotest interest in her made Peta want him all the more.

She was consumed with a hunger she had never felt before. She craved to feel his body against hers, she desperately wanted his kisses, and the longer time went on the more she desired him.

It was becoming an impossible situation.

'How much longer do you plan on staying here?' she asked as they sat outside one evening after the boys were in bed. It was quiet save for the rustle in the trees and the occasional squawk of a bird. 'You can't ignore your business interests for ever.' In fact she was surprised that he had stayed away from them for so long.

'Everything is being well looked after,' he told her

brusquely. 'And I intend to remain here for as long as is necessary.'

'How will you know when the kidnapper has lost interest? What if he's staking out your mother's house, waiting for you to return? What if he kidnaps your mother instead?'

This latter was obviously something that had never occurred to him, for his eyes snapped open. Then he gave a harsh laugh. 'Kidnapping my mother would be their worst nightmare. She'd give them hell. They'd soon realise their mistake.'

'Whatever, we can't stay here indefinitely,' she said.

'Getting fed up, are we?' he asked with a further flash of his magnificent chestnut eyes.

Peta shook her head, auburn hair flying. 'No, but I imagine the boys will get bored soon. There's only so much to do here.'

'They're not showing any signs.'

She shrugged but didn't answer. It was a pointless conversation. She should never have started it.

'I think that you're the one who's finding life dull,' he said softly. And, when there was still no response from her, 'Perhaps it's because I'm not paying you any attention?'

His words had her sucking in a horrified breath and she jumped to her feet and walked a few paces away. Was he saying that he was deliberately leaving her alone? That it wasn't because of what she'd said about his wife?

'It's what you want, isn't it?' he asked.

'Of course.'

'And yet it makes you look miserable.'

'It's not because of—'

Her words were cut off when Andreas whirled her to

face him and his mouth claimed hers in a kiss that sent
her spinning into space. Yes, this was what she wanted.
This!

She felt herself melting, every one of her senses leaping into action. The exciting male smell of him filled her
nostrils, teasing and tormenting, making her wriggle
against him, inciting him to deepen the kiss, his tongue
plunging and thrilling.

He tasted good, oh, so good. This was definitely what
she had wanted, had needed, even, over the last few
days. She had thought he would never kiss her again,
but apparently he had been as miserable as she, and now
he was unable to contain his hunger.

When she dared to open her eyes he was looking at
her with a smouldering intensity that tightened every one
of her muscles and sent shock wave reeling after shock
wave. He lifted his mouth for a fraction of a second to
utter gruffly, 'You're beautiful.'

And so was he! So was he. Her answer was a mew
of satisfaction, and when one hand crept beneath the
hem of her cotton top to slide purposefully towards her
breast Peta drew in a deep breath of anticipation—and
held it. She fitted into the palm of his hand perfectly,
but it was not until his thumb grazed across her already
erect and expectant nipple that she expelled the air from
her body and gave a further cry of pleasure.

Whether he was using her or not, it suddenly didn't
matter. She would be a fool to deny what her body so
badly wanted. As she involuntarily ground her hips
against his she felt the full, exciting extent of his arousal,
heard the groan deep in his throat, and gave an answering whimper as his hand tightened over her breast.

'This is no good,' he declared edgily. 'I've been patient long enough.' And with an expertise that sent her

mind reeling he whipped her white top over her head and flicked the clasp on her bra. In a matter of seconds her breasts were exposed to his eager eyes.

'Ben and Nikos!' she exclaimed. 'What if—?'

'They're fast asleep,' he assured her, leading her indoors, laying her down on the couch so that he could kneel in front of her. When he began an assault on her breasts with fingers and teeth and tongue Peta very soon grew past caring. This was heaven. This was the stuff dreams were made of. He was quickly transporting her to another world.

She lay back and wallowed in the sensations he was creating. She felt a desperate, urgent, aching hunger to be made love to. No man had ever aroused her to such depths. His tongue flicked the sensitive nub of her breast, his teeth grazed and incited, and she moved uncontrollably beneath him.

'Let's go to bed,' he growled, lifting his head to look into the deep ocean-blue of her eyes.

Peta saw her own raw hunger mirrored on his face. And hunger won. She gave a faint nod and allowed him to lift her effortlessly into his arms. As he walked slowly into the next room he trailed kisses across her brow and over her nose. He kissed each eyelid in turn, each eyebrow, and by the time he put her down her heart was pounding fit to burst.

The vague notion that she was making a grave mistake entered her mind, but she dismissed it instantly and when he kissed her again she entwined her arms around the back of his neck and held him close.

'This is what you want?' he asked roughly.

'Yes!' she whispered urgently. 'Yes, yes, yes!'

'There'll be no regrets?' He began to ease her skirt down over her hips, Peta obligingly lifting her body.

'None at all.'

'You're sure, now?' It was the turn of her panties next, brief triangles of white lace that hid almost nothing.

Peta was beyond answering. Not very long ago she would have felt embarrassed lying in front of Andreas stark naked, but there was something very erotic about having him undress her, especially when he began to strip off his own clothes, too.

When he lay beside her it was not only a joining of bodies but also a joining of senses. They were each hotly aroused, each hungry for the pleasure that lay ahead.

His hands and mouth explored and tormented every inch. 'You're incredible,' he muttered as she heaved and wriggled beneath his touch.

She was fast losing any semblance of self-control, touching him now, stroking and kissing his nipples, his chest; doing to him what he was doing to her. Bodies melded, bodies overheated, bodies grew desperate with need.

He took her hand, urged her to hold him, to feel for herself what she was doing to him. Her touch was almost his undoing. He moved himself over her. She spread her legs instinctively, obligingly. 'Are you sure?' he asked hoarsely. 'There'll be no going back once I—'

'I'm sure, Andreas,' she groaned. 'Take me. Now! Make me yours.'

She felt him hesitate and knew that she had once again spoken without thinking. *Make me yours.* She would never be his. Not in the true sense of the word. He would never ask her to marry him. This was pure sex—pure, unadulterated sex. Two consenting adults behaving in the way that man and woman had since time immemorial.

Now was the time to back out, now was the time to put a stop to it, but she couldn't. Her need was too great. His need was too great.

Already he was entering her, already she was rising to meet him, muscles clenching, holding, urging. It was all and more than she had expected and the final climax lifted them both to another plane. She couldn't help crying out and Andreas groaned his satisfaction too as they collapsed in a heap of slick sweat and pleasure.

But their breathing had not even returned to normal before Nikos came running into the room. 'Daddy, where's Ben?' he asked. 'Where have you taken him?'

CHAPTER TEN

'BEN isn't here, son,' answered Andreas, pushing himself up on one elbow. 'Are you sure you weren't dreaming? I've not been in your room.'

'Yes, you have, I saw you,' Nikos insisted. 'You told him to be quiet. I was awake because I heard noises.'

Peta started to shake as the horror of the situation began to sink in. Andreas shot to his feet and tugged on his trousers. 'How long ago was this, Nikos?'

'Not long. Where is Ben? What's happened?'

'I don't know, but I intend to find out. Peta, you stay here with Nikos.' He was out of the room in two bounds.

Outside, Andreas paused for a second or two, listening. The air up here in the mountains was perfectly still; every little noise carried. But he heard nothing except the scurrying of a tiny animal in the undergrowth.

But then, as his ears became more attuned, he heard what he had most feared—the faint drone of an engine. He swore loudly, dashed back inside for his car keys and was out again in seconds. He ignored Peta's demands that he take her with him, even though he knew what she must be going through. And it was all his fault, dammit.

If he hadn't weakened none of this would have happened. If he hadn't listened to the urges of his body Ben would be safe now. And Lord knew what the kidnapper would do when he realised he had the wrong boy.

It wasn't yet completely dark and he careered down

the mountainside with little heed for his own safety. He needed to catch up with the kidnapper before he reached the main road, because if he didn't he would have no way of knowing which way he had gone.

Peta would never forgive him if anything happened to her son. Ben was her whole life; she idolised him. She'd even shown him, Andreas, the error of his ways. Nikos had almost always been left to his own devices, or to the care of his nanny, before he'd met Peta. Through her he'd realised how much Nikos was missing out on a father's influence. He'd made a pact with himself that in future he'd be different.

Andreas came to the bottom of the track and there was no sign of the other vehicle as he slithered to a halt. Which way should he go? Left or right? He tried the listening technique again but there was other traffic on the road. He took a guess at left, but after a few miles realised it was like searching for a needle in a haystack. He had no idea what sort of vehicle he was looking for.

By the time he got back up the mountain Peta was frantic. She practically fell on him as he climbed out of his vehicle, her face crumpling when she saw that he was alone.

'I'm sorry,' he said, holding her so tightly against him that she couldn't breathe. 'I've done everything I can. It's now in the hands of the police.'

The tears that she had bravely held back in front of Nikos streamed unchecked down her cheeks. She blamed herself. It had been sheer madness giving in to Andreas, except that she'd been equally guilty of wanting to feed her need. They'd been so intent on themselves that they'd heard nothing of what was going on around them.

Quite clearly the kidnapper had been watching the house. He'd probably been staking it out for days, waiting for the right opportunity. He'd seen Andreas half undress her, he'd watched as she was carried into the house, probably even leered through the window as Andreas had sucked and tormented her breasts. It didn't bear thinking about.

And when they'd gone into the bedroom he'd taken his chance, knowing that they were too carried away to hear anything that was going on.

'Oh, God, Andreas,' she sobbed. 'If anything happens to Ben I'll kill myself.'

'Don't talk like that. Nothing will happen to him,' he assured her gently, pulling a clean white handkerchief out of his pocket and pressing it into her hand. 'When they realise they've got the wrong little guy he'll be released, you'll see.'

But Peta wasn't convinced. 'They might not,' she sniffed. 'They might—get rid of him. They could do anything.' Every worst-case scenario was running through her mind.

'The most they'll do is demand money, the same as they would if they'd kidnapped Nikos. It's all they're after, Peta. I know what they're like.'

'How do you know?' she demanded, dabbing her eyes ineffectually because the tears wouldn't stop coming.

His mouth tightened grimly. 'Believe me, I do; it's the way these men work. The police will be here shortly, and after that we're going back down to my mother's.'

'You—you said we'd be s-safe here,' she blubbered.

'I thought we would. I'm so sorry, Peta.' His arms tightened around her once again, trying to reassure her but having little effect. 'I'll do everything I can to ensure Ben is returned to you safely.'

Meaning he'd pay the ransom. Which was the least he could do under the circumstances, she thought bitterly. And yet even as she leaned into his body his strength supported her. The warmth of him consoled her. She had no right to blame Andreas. He couldn't have been more concerned had it been Nikos.

'Oughtn't we to stay?' she asked huskily. 'If—if they're going to return Ben this is where they'll bring him, won't they? And if they send a ransom note it will also come here.'

'I expect so,' he agreed, 'but I think it's no place for you to be now. There'll be a twenty-four-hour guard, don't worry.'

The next few hours passed in a blur. It was embarrassing having to tell the two policemen what they'd been doing while Ben was being kidnapped, even though their faces remained impassive. And they assured her that at first light someone would be back to search the area around the house. She was still tearful when they eventually returned to his parent's home.

Mrs Papadakis, having been warned beforehand what had happened, couldn't have been nicer. The frostiness had gone, the haughtiness had gone, and she hugged Peta as though she was someone very special. 'My son, he tells me about it. I am so sorry that this has happened to you in my country. I hope Ben will be returned to you very soon. Meantime you must not worry. Everything is being done that can be done.'

Peta nodded, not trusting herself to speak.

'I think you should rest; I think you should try to sleep.'

'I won't sleep,' she insisted, shaking her head, 'not until Ben's been found.'

'At least lie down, child. Andreas, take Peta to her room.'

Nikos had already been dispatched to bed and reluctantly Peta allowed herself to be helped. Andreas sat down on the edge of the bed with her. 'When this is all over I'm going to make it up to you, I promise.'

'When this is all over you won't see me again,' she assured him fiercely, ignoring the startled look in his eyes. She had made up her mind that she was going back to England and looking for a new job. Living with Andreas was too dangerous. Not only because of what had happened to Ben but for her own peace of mind, too. She simply wasn't the type who could indulge in an affair. 'If I hadn't allowed myself to be manipulated by you none of this would have happened,' she pointed out. 'I should never have taken the nanny's job.'

'Don't talk like that, Peta,' he said gently. 'It's my fault; I take full responsibility. I more or less said that if you didn't you'd be out of work. It was cruel of me, but I just knew you'd be perfect. I never expected this to happen.' He punched his thigh, not once but several times. 'Here was I, trying to protect Nikos, and now, because some incompetent stuffed up, you are out of your mind with worry. I hold myself entirely responsible.'

'We're both to blame,' amended Peta wearily.

'Who'd have thought that he'd have the audacity to enter the house while we were all there?'

'We left the door open.'

He nodded grimly. 'We were too wrapped up in ourselves.'

'I'd like you to leave,' she said now, lying back on the bed, utterly weary but knowing that she wouldn't sleep, not until Ben was safely returned.

She was mistaken. The moment she closed her eyes she fell asleep, but it wasn't a restful sleep. She dreamt of Ben, dreamt that his kidnappers were torturing him, and she thrashed about on the bed, calling to him, telling him that she was coming. She was woken by Andreas gently shaking her. 'It's all right, Peta, it's just a bad dream.'

'Ben?' She sat bolt upright.

'No news yet, I'm afraid.'

'What time is it? How long have I been asleep?' She felt guilty for daring to drop off while her son's life was in danger.

'It's midday.'

Her eyes shot wide. 'And you've heard nothing?'

'Not yet.'

'No ransom note?'

'No.'

'What's taking so long? I want my son; he'll be terrified. He's never been away from me before.'

'I know.' He held her gently, a finger stroking the hair away from her face, cradling her; trying to soothe her. And it helped—a little! She liked the feel of him; he was strong and powerful and comforting; he'd take care of her; he'd help her find Ben, come hell or high water.

She leaned into him, felt his strength become her strength. 'What can we do?' she asked clearly.

'We're having lunch here, my mother has ordered it, and then I'm going to see the police again. Find out what progress has been made.'

'I'm coming with you,' she said firmly.

She ate only a mouthful of fish and half a grilled tomato before declaring she'd had enough. 'I can't eat while I don't know where Ben is. Do you think he's being looked after, Andreas? Do you think he'll come to any harm?'

Before he could answer Anna tapped on the door and brought in an envelope, which she passed to Andreas, speaking quickly in her own language.

He ripped it open and his eyes hardened as he scanned the contents. Silently he handed it to Peta. It was a demand for the million pounds to be paid in English currency.

'I wonder if he realises that he's got the wrong boy,' mused Andreas.

'Would it make any difference?' she demanded. 'We gave a pretty good indication of how close we are.' Her cheeks flushed as she recalled what they'd been up to.

'I know it's no time to tell you,' he said gruffly, 'but you were magnificent, Peta.'

'No, it's not the right time,' she snapped. 'What are we going to do about this?' She waved the note in front of his face.

'Take it to the police, of course.'

'He says not to.'

'Don't they always?'

'I don't want to do anything that will jeopardise Ben's safety.'

'I wish I knew who was doing this to me,' he said grimly.

'To *you*?' queried Peta. 'What the hell have you got to worry about?' She wished he hadn't reminded her how good it had been in bed. As a matter of fact she never wanted to be reminded of it again. It was a moment in her life that she would regret for as long as she lived.

'Do you think that because he isn't my son I don't

care?' he questioned, brown eyes suddenly hard. 'Hell, Peta, you should know me better than that.'

'I don't know what to think any more,' she replied. 'All I want is my son back.'

The next few days were sheer hell. The waiting drove Peta almost insane. Andreas was a tower of strength, but she couldn't help thinking that if it hadn't been for him none of this would have happened. And she was firm in her resolve that after it was over she would get well out of his life.

Mrs Papadakis walked into the room one day when Peta was sobbing into Andreas's shoulder; his mother motioned him to leave. She sat next to Peta on the sofa and talked calmly and soothingly until finally she stopped crying.

'I can't bear this any longer,' Peta whimpered.

'I know, child. I know, but you must be patient. Let me tell you something.'

Peta scrubbed ineffectually at her face, knowing it would do nothing to help the redness of her nose and eyes. Oh, Lord, when was this nightmare going to end?

'I know how you are feeling. Andreas's brother, he was kidnapped when he was about Ben's age.'

'Oh!' Peta clapped a hand to her mouth. 'Andreas never told me.' Actually, it was just as well; she'd have been paranoid. And it was clearly the reason why he hadn't initially told his mother about the threats. He'd wanted to protect her, to save unhappy memories flooding back. And now she must be hurting, too, reliving that painful time. It accounted for the way her attitude had changed so dramatically. Here was another woman going through exactly the same trauma.

'It would seem,' went on the older woman, 'that anyone who has great wealth is a ready-made target for such ruthless people. I wanted my husband to pay; I would have given up everything, *everything* to get Christos back. But my husband, he thought he knew best. He did not tell the police; he thought he could handle it himself. He did not even tell me when he went to meet the kidnapper. He almost paid for it with his life. Fortunately I got my son back, and my husband; he healed in time. So you see, you must be patient, you must let Andreas and the police work out the best plan of action. It is the only way you can ensure both your son's and my son's safety.'

Through the blur of fresh tears Peta saw that Mrs Papadakis was crying, too.

Finally, after days of waiting, the kidnapper phoned Andreas, giving a time and place where he wanted the money deposited. 'The kid's told me he's not your son, but it makes no difference. One boy is as good as another. And since he's the son of a girl who would appear, from what I saw, to be very special to you—' there was a sickening leer in his voice '—it will be in your best interests to pay. Let the girl bring the money.'

As Peta carried the bag containing the ransom her heart threatened to jump out of her chest. It beat so hard that it was painful and she could hardly breathe. She was supposed to put the bag into a railway-station deposit box—she had the key the kidnapper had sent in her pocket—but she felt like dropping the case now and running. This was the most dangerous thing she'd ever had to do.

Except that it was Ben's life she was carrying in her hand. A million pounds for Ben's life, and Andreas was prepared to pay it! If all went according to plan they'd catch the kidnapper and he'd get his money back. But

if it didn't, if she got Ben back but no money, then
Andreas would be out of pocket. She would indeed be
indebted to him then. She wouldn't be able to walk
away.

As she walked into the station Peta knew that she must
remain calm. She mustn't draw attention to herself. But
she couldn't help wondering whether the kidnapper was
watching. Her eyes darted this way and that but no one
took any notice of the auburn-haired English girl in a
flowered dress and sun-hat, with a battered briefcase
tucked under her arm.

She almost expected a gun in her back as she deposited the case, then scolded herself for letting her imagination run away. It was a relief when she was back outside in the hot Greek sunshine, and an even bigger relief
when Andreas drew up in his car. 'My brave darling,'
he said as she virtually fell into it.

Peta closed her eyes and rested her head on his shoulder for a few seconds. But it wasn't over yet. Already
plain-clothes policemen would have moved into the station. The waiting game had begun in earnest.

Twenty-four hours went by and the money hadn't
been collected. Peta was inconsolable. And then came
the call they were waiting for.

Andreas raced out to his car, Peta close on his heels,
and as they reached the station they were in time to see
a short, stocky man with light ginger hair being led away
by two unsmiling policemen. The man looked across at
Andreas with hatred in his eyes. Behind them a police-
woman was holding Ben's hand.

As soon as he saw his mother he flew across to her.
Peta's relief was so overwhelming that she burst into
tears, and it was a moment or two before she realised

that Andreas actually knew the man who had stolen her child.

'Craig Eden, no less,' he said.

'You know this man?' asked one of the policemen.

'He knows me all right,' declared the kidnapper fiercely. 'He took everything I owned. Left me with not a penny to support my wife and family.'

Andreas shook his head. 'That's not strictly true, Craig.'

'Seems a pretty reasonable description of the facts to me,' he growled.

'Your company was in trouble. I bought it. I gave you a fair price. End of story.'

'A fair price? Is that what you call it?' sneered Craig Eden, his top lip curled, his eyes brilliantly hard. 'You didn't buy my debts, did you? No, you were too crafty for that. By the time I'd finished paying out there was nothing left. Have you found out what it feels like to be afraid? To be haunted by a fear night and day? It's what I felt when I thought my house was going to be taken off me. You broke me, Andreas Papadakis, and I saw no reason why I should live on the breadline while you lead a life of luxury.'

'Except that it didn't work out, did it?' scorned Andreas. 'Breaking the law never does. You're not quite as clever as you thought you were.'

As the police led the man away Andreas put his arms around Peta and Ben and for a moment none of them spoke, the sheer relief of the moment so overwhelming. Ben was crying, tears streamed down Peta's cheeks, and when Andreas finally said, 'Let's get into the car,' she heard a break in his voice, too.

On the journey back to Andreas's mother's house Peta sat in the back with Ben, her arm tightly around him, never wanting to let him go again. 'Did the man hurt you, sweetheart?' she asked gently.

'No, Mummy, he was a kind man.'

'Did he feed you?'

'Of course. I had lots to eat. I asked him why he had taken me to his house. I told him I wanted to go home. I said that if he didn't take me back Andreas would come and get me. Andreas, were you really going to pay all that money for me?'

'Yes, I was, Ben.'

'Wow, you must be very rich. Are you the richest man in the world?'

Andreas looked at Peta in the interior mirror and smiled gently. 'Yes, I think I must be. If not the richest, the most fortunate.'

It had taken one small child and one very beautiful young woman to make him realise that it was time he let go of the past and got on with his future. He loved Peta. He loved her with all his heart. The discovery was a glorious, uplifting experience. It was as though all the weight of the world had been lifted from his shoulders. He had lost so much in his life that he couldn't bear it if he lost Peta now.

And yet, looking at her in the mirror, he could see that now wasn't the time to tell her. All her love was for her son at this moment, and it probably always would be. She had told him more than once that there was no place in her life for a man.

Somehow he would have to change her mind.

CHAPTER ELEVEN

'YOU deserve a holiday,' Andreas said softly. 'It's time to relax and enjoy yourself once more.'

It was a few days after Ben's release. They'd all, including his mother, talked about nothing else except the kidnapping. About the way Craig Eden had tried to play on their feelings. The way it had been a rerun of Christos's disappearance. The fear the whole thing had engendered. In its own way it had made a deep impact on all three of them.

'We could leave the boys with my mother and—'

'How can you even suggest such a thing?' Peta demanded, blue eyes incredulous. 'Don't you know what I've gone through because of you? I want to go home,' she stormed, shaking her head violently. 'And when I say home I mean back to my own place. You'll have to find another nanny for Nikos. I can't do it any more.'

The shock that ran through him felt like a rocket out of control; it ricocheted through every space in his body. She wanted to leave him! Move out of his life altogether! For the first time in his life he was at a loss for words. 'Why?'

'Do you need to ask?' Her gorgeous eyes flashed, her lovely lips curled, twisting his stomach as he looked at them. 'But apart from the obvious,' she added, 'I'm not cut out to be a nanny. I'm not even sure that I want to do office work any longer.'

In other words she wanted to be free of him! It was like a knife stabbing into his chest. 'So what do you

156

want?' he asked, aware of the gruffness to his tone. 'You need to support Ben. I pay you excellent wages. You won't do better anywhere.' Lord, it sounded as though he was pleading with her, and he was. He couldn't afford to let her go.

'Money isn't everything,' she riposted.

'That isn't what you said to me before.'

'I hadn't discovered then that living with you was like living on the edge of an active volcano. And don't try to change my mind, Andreas, because you'll be wasting your time.'

'Very well, we'll go back,' he said reluctantly, even though he wasn't sure whether letting Peta have her own way was the wisest thing to do. Ought he to tell her now that he loved her? No, it had to be when she was in the right frame of mind. She would think he was using it as a tool to persuade her to stay. She wouldn't believe him.

He was aware that she deeply regretted letting him make love to her, that she constantly blamed herself for Ben being kidnapped; it was a guilt she was going to live with for the rest of her life. But didn't she realise that he felt equally guilty? He couldn't have felt worse had it been his own son. And he wanted to make it up to her. He had thought that a holiday would be the answer, the perfect antidote. Clearly wishful thinking on his part.

Peta had slowly and surely wormed her way into his heart. She had shown him the error of his ways where Nikos was concerned; she had made him see that there was life after the death of a loved one. The trouble was she didn't want a man in her life. She was happy living alone. Occasionally she forgot herself and let her emotions ride high, but almost immediately she regretted it and shut herself back into her ice palace.

Was time and patience the answer? Or should he simply let her go?

But he knew he couldn't do that. If he had to go back to the beginning and pursue her all over again then he would. He would do it differently this time. He would do it the old-fashioned way, with flowers and gifts, and he would never, ever use his authority on her again.

'My mother will be extremely disappointed,' he told her now. 'I think she was looking forward to having the boys.'

Peta's eyes flashed her indignation. 'You spoke to her before me?'

'I needed to make sure she'd have them before I asked you.'

'You mean you thought that you'd *tell* me what we were going to do, the same as always. You never consider anyone else, do you, Andreas? You make up your mind and everyone's supposed to fall in. Well, not this girl, not any longer. I've had enough of following orders. In future I'm going to do what *I* want to do. How soon can we go home?'

He was stunned anew by her outburst. He hadn't realised quite how strongly she felt. He was very tempted to answer in kind. But that would get him nowhere with a woman like Peta. Patience and consideration was the name of the game now.

'I'll make the arrangements,' he said.

Nikos and Ben were as disappointed as he was, and made their feelings very clear, but Peta was adamant.

It was late when they arrived in Southampton. Peta had hardly spoken on the flight. She'd sunk into a world of her own. Most situations he could handle, but for once he didn't know what to do.

'Your property was let on a monthly lease,' he reminded her as he drove to his own house, 'so it might be a little while before you can go back.'

Peta's eyes shot wide. 'I can't wait a whole month.'

'I promise I won't let any harm come to Ben again.'

'It's not that,' she snapped.

No, it was him she didn't want to live with. Because he'd made love to her she'd decided that she wanted nothing more to do with him. She felt that he'd overstepped the mark, even though she herself had been willing. It had been a turning point in their relationship, one that she didn't want to face. That and the fact that Ben had been kidnapped while they were making love. The two would be associated in her mind for ever.

Peta was afraid. Afraid that if she was forced to live in the same house as Andreas for any length of time she would give in to the yearnings of her body. There had to be another solution. She could, of course, spend the time with her parents—they would love to have her and Ben—but she didn't see that as the answer either. Her mother would ask far too many pertinent questions, ones that she wasn't yet ready to answer.

The following morning she was relieved to find that Andreas had already left for Linam's when she got up. The boys played happily with their Scalextric and she helped Bess with the washing. Not that the housekeeper wanted her to, but she needed something to take her mind off Andreas and the love that she felt for him.

'Does Andreas ever mention his wife?' she tentatively asked the other woman.

'Quite often,' she admitted with the widest of smiles. 'There's no escaping the fact that he used to adore that woman. I can't see him ever marrying again. Pity, though. It's all wrong that a man like him should remain single for ever. Why do you ask? Do you fancy him yourself?'

Peta turned her head away so that Bess wouldn't see the quick colour that warmed her cheeks. 'Heavens, no. He's too demanding. Not my type at all.'

'What is your type?' asked the housekeeper, nothing but warm interest on her face.

'I'll know when I meet him,' returned Peta quickly. 'Shall I go and peg these out?' She now knew for sure that Andreas had no serious intentions where she was concerned. An affair was most definitely all that he wanted. It wasn't worth the heartache.

When Andreas returned he was thankfully not alone. 'Peta, I'd like you to meet my brother, Christos. Christos, this is Peta.'

'Nikos's nanny,' informed Peta, taking his hand. She saw Andreas's frown but ignored it. She felt it necessary to make it perfectly clear what her position was in this household.

Christos's handshake was firm and warm, his smile full of genuine interest. He was a couple of inches shorter than Andreas but with the same black hair, although his eyes were a lighter brown and his face less aggressively male. 'I've heard a lot about you from the staff at Linam's. They were sorry to see you go.'

'I was given no choice.' She heard Andreas's indrawn breath but she didn't look at him. 'And I won't be Nikos's nanny for much longer either. I'm looking for work elsewhere.'

'You are?' Christos showed his surprise. 'Why's that? Doesn't my brother pay you enough?' It was meant as a joke but Andreas didn't smile.

'It's not the money. I just don't like being a nanny.'

'You could go back to Linam's. They'd welcome you with open arms.'

He had more of an accent than his brother and she found it very attractive.

Andreas grunted something that sounded like an affirmative but Peta knew that she would never work for him again. She wanted to distance herself as far away as possible.

'Are you joining us for dinner?' asked Christos.

'Of course she is,' said Andreas before she could speak.

There he went again, telling her what to do. Her blue eyes flashed daggers in his direction and if Christos hadn't been there she would have told him exactly what she thought of him. Instead she smiled sweetly at his brother. 'It would be my pleasure.'

During the meal Christos seemed unable to take his eyes off her. 'Tell me all about yourself,' he said. 'My brother here has been remarkably reticent where you're concerned. All I know is that you have an eight-year-old son who was kidnapped. You must have been out of your mind with worry.'

Peta nodded. 'Indeed I was. They were the blackest days of my life.' Blacker even than when Joe had dumped her, and that had been bad enough. 'But all's well that ends well,' she added brightly.

'Do you have any brothers or sisters?'

'No, there's just me—and my parents. They live in Cornwall.'

'Do they know about the kidnapping?' He'd stopped eating and was giving her his undivided attention.

'Goodness, no,' she said with a half-laugh. 'I rang today to let them know I'm back but I didn't want to worry them.'

'They'd think Andreas wasn't looking after you properly, is that it?' he asked with a grin and a sideways glance at his brother.

Andreas scowled, and the longer she talked with Christos the blacker his face got. Peta pretended not to notice. She liked Christos. He was easy to talk to and genuinely friendly and interested. She couldn't see him ever barking orders the way Andreas did. She would like to bet that he got on well with the staff at Linam's.

'How do you like working in England?' she asked.

'Very much. I think I'd like to live here. How about letting me take over Linam's altogether, Andreas?'

Andreas shook his head decisively. 'No go, Christos. I thought you were eager to return to Greece?'

Christos looked at Peta and his dark eyes were meaningful. 'I hadn't reckoned on meeting this charming young lady. How about letting me take you out tomorrow night, Peta?'

'I don't think that would be a good idea,' growled Andreas.

Christos shot him a quick, startled look. 'Am I treading on toes here? I had no idea. I'm—'

'Of course not,' said Peta swiftly. 'And, yes, I'd love to come out with you.' Quite why she had said that she didn't know. But Andreas didn't own her. Why shouldn't she go out with Christos? It would be a fun, no-strings-attached night. She'd be able to relax and let her hair down—something she was finding it increasingly difficult to do with Andreas.

Christos smiled but Andreas's eyes were hard and narrowed, and later that evening he came to Peta's room. She was undressed and ready for bed when he pushed open the door. He didn't even knock, and she didn't have to look at his face to know what he'd come for. Every muscle in her body grew tense.

'What game are you playing?' he demanded. 'What made you say you'd go out with Christos?'

'Why shouldn't I?' she asked with the characteristic lift of her chin. 'You don't own me.'

'I don't own you, no, but I thought we meant something to each other.'

'Then you thought wrong, Andreas. I should never have given in to you. It was a huge mistake. I don't want to get involved with anyone. I thought you knew that.'

'Not ever?' he asked quietly.

'Not ever.'

'Then why are you going out with Christos?'

'Because he looks as though he'll be fun. I need a little lightness in my life at this moment.'

'He fancies you.'

'Nonsense,' she retorted. 'He's only just met me.'

'That doesn't stop it. I too fancied you from the word go. It's a male thing. It's what develops from it that's the problem.'

A shock wave sizzled through Peta's body. Andreas had fancied her from the beginning? He'd sure had a funny way of showing it. He'd done nothing but bark and bawl at her from the very second she'd set foot in his office.

'Let me tell you,' she said, eyeing him boldly, 'nothing will develop between me and Christos. You, above all people, should know that.'

'I know that when a girl meets the right man nothing can stop it.'

'And you think Christos might be the right man for me?'

'Who's to know?' he asked with a very foreign shrug.

'Are you jealous, Andreas?' She knew that he couldn't be, but what other possible reason was there for his behaviour?

'I simply want to make sure that you know what you're doing. Christos is a charmer. Make sure you don't get your fingers burnt.'

And Andreas didn't think he was a charmer himself? Heavens, he had charmed the socks off her. He had made her fall so deeply in love with him that no man would ever interest her again. Christos was merely a diversion, someone to take her mind off her aching heart.

She closed her eyes. 'There's no chance of me doing that,' she said in a soft whisper. And when she opened them again he had taken a step towards her.

Peta backed away, felt the bed behind her legs, and knew that she had nowhere to run. Panic spread through her. 'If you wouldn't mind I'd like to go to bed,' she said sharply.

A slow smile spread across his face. 'That's the best invitation I've had in a long time.'

It took a few seconds for her to realise that he was teasing. A few seconds in which her heart did several somersaults and her legs threatened to give way. Andreas, teasing! That was a first. 'I meant alone,' she stressed.

His smile widened. 'Sleep well, then, my beautiful Peta. I think the boys should go back to school now. I'll take Nikos in the morning and explain to his headmaster. I think you should take Ben.'

Peta nodded.

'And you'll pick them up after school?'

'Of course,' she answered swiftly.

'So I'll see you at breakfast?'

'Yes.'

'May I kiss you goodnight?'

He was asking! Unbelievable! How could she refuse? But fear filled her heart as she gave a little nod.

She need not have worried. It was the lightest of kisses, the sort she gave Ben. A gentle hug and then he was gone, and she was left wondering. Had he taken her at her word? Had he accepted that their little romance was over? Was her time here not going to be the ordeal she'd expected?

As she crawled into bed Peta could find no answer to these questions. Andreas wasn't the type to give in, not when he'd set his sights on something. Even if she couldn't move back into her house maybe she ought to find somewhere else to live temporarily.

She discovered over breakfast that Christos had been living in Andreas's house while they were in Greece. Not that it should have surprised her, but it was something she'd never thought about. And now, as they tucked in to one of Bess's cooked breakfasts, he looked at her with a warmness that made her glance covertly at Andreas.

He was, as she had expected, frowning his disapproval. His eyes were on his brother, not her, as if trying to work out how serious Christos was.

'You haven't forgotten our dinner date tonight?' he asked, pausing as he speared a slice of sausage.

'Of course not.' She glanced again at Andreas and his eyes were on her now. 'Why don't you join us, Andreas?' she suggested, half joking, half serious.

'And tread on my brother's toes?' he asked lightly. 'You know what they say about three being a crowd.'

Christos had frowned when she extended the invitation, now he gave a relieved smile. 'Let Andreas find his own girl,' he said. 'I've never known him to be short. It's about time, brother dear, that you married again. It's wrong for Nikos to keep having nannies. Although,' he added, looking disarmingly at Peta, 'if they're all like Peta then I can see why you do it. A ready-made source of attractive females on tap. You've got it made.'

'You don't know what the hell you're talking about,' snapped Andreas, scraping his chair back from the table. 'I'll go and see if Nikos is ready.' The boys were eating their breakfast in the kitchen, and even though Peta had declared that her place was with them Andreas had insisted that she join him and his brother.

After Andreas had left the room Christos raised his brows. 'What was that all about? He's one seriously touchy man since his return.'

Peta shrugged. She didn't want to get into a discussion about his brother.

'Are you sure there's nothing between you and him? He seems very prickly where you're concerned.'

'Absolutely nothing,' she retorted. 'He's my employer, that's all.'

Christos raised his brows but said no more, although it was clear that he didn't entirely believe her, and she couldn't blame him. She'd been a little too vehement in her denial. And when she left to check on Ben he said, 'Is it still on for tonight?'

'Why shouldn't it be?' she asked sharply from the doorway.

'No reason; just checking.'

But when evening came and Andreas watched them leave Peta began to wish that she hadn't been so eager to accept Christos's invitation. Andreas knew, and she knew, that she was doing it to spite him, and when she returned she would more than likely be subjected to a full-scale interrogation.

'Are you sure you're happy about this?' asked Christos as they set off.

'Perfectly,' she answered smoothly. Except that inside she was filled with several conflicting emotions. She wanted to do this; she wanted to show Andreas that she didn't belong to him and that she had no intention of getting involved with him on a long-term basis. At the same time she wanted to prove to herself that she could date other men and be happy about it. She wanted to confirm that she was a free agent. Except that, being in love with Andreas, she would never be that. Not ever again for as long as she lived. It was a daunting thought.

'Because I believe,' said Christos quietly, 'that there is something going on between Andreas and yourself. I know you've denied it, and my brother won't even speak about you, but neither of you is doing a very good job of concealing your real feelings.'

Peta looked at him wide-eyed, an uncomfortable feeling stirring in her stomach. 'What are you saying?'

'That I think you're in love with each other, but you're either both too stupid to see it, or you have your own reasons for denying it.'

The uncomfortable feeling turned into chilling horror. Surely he couldn't see? 'Andreas doesn't love me,' she scorned.

'You think not?'

'I know not.'

'What makes you so sure?'

'Because of his wife. No one will ever take her place.'

They stopped at a set of traffic lights and he turned to her. 'I used to think that, but since he's met you there's something very different about him. I think he's finally let go.'

Peta's eyes met and held Christos's, then she turned away. 'I can't accept that,' she said. 'He's never given me any reason to believe that he loves me.'

'My brother is not the sort of man who can talk easily about his emotions.' The lights changed and they were off again. 'He can talk on any subject under the sun except love. Some men are like that, Peta. Now, me, I see no reason not to tell a woman that she's beautiful and I adore her and that I'm falling in love with her.' He looked briefly across at her as he spoke and Peta felt a twinge of unease. What if he was trying to tell her something? Things were complicated enough without him adding to it.

'So how about you?' he went on. 'Do you love Andreas?'

Peta hesitated a fraction too long before attempting an answer.

'You give yourself away,' he said on a deep sigh. 'And I'm sorry, because I'd hoped that I was in with a chance.'

'I'm sorry, too,' Peta whispered. This whole conversation was extremely painful. 'Do you still want to take me out to dinner?'

'Of course. Let's give Andreas something to think about.' He reached out and touched her hand and Peta smiled. Perhaps this evening wouldn't be too bad after all.

Andreas couldn't relax. In his mind's eye he kept seeing Peta and Christos walking out of the house together, driving off together, eating dinner in a cosy restaurant, still together. Their conversation would be intimate;

Christos would work his charm on her. He was very good at that, his little brother. While Andreas had been building up his business empire Christos had been captivating the girls. It was surprising he'd never married. He'd been forever coming home declaring that he was in love.

And the instant he'd set eyes on Peta he'd been knocked off his feet. And he, Andreas, had more or less given him *carte blanche* to do as he liked by refusing to discuss his own feelings. He was a fool. He was his own worst enemy. What if Peta fell hook, line and sinker for Christos? How would he be able to win her over then?

He paced from room to room, upstairs, downstairs, upstairs, downstairs. He tried to work at his computer but found it impossible. More pacing, more cursing. He had a photograph of Maria in his bedroom and he looked at it for a long, sober minute. God, but she was beautiful. His stomach churned simply looking at her and he felt the prick of tears at the backs of his eyes. She was an exotic beauty with none of Peta's coyness and delicate English-rose charm. There was a whole world of difference between the two women. And he loved them both!

As he continued holding the picture and looking into Maria's sultry brown eyes he felt her speaking to him. He heard her telling him that the time had come to get on with his life, that he could mourn her no longer. And she told him to hurry or he would lose the woman he had now fallen in love with. *She'll be good for you, Andreas, good for you and good for Nikos. Take her with my blessing.*

Take her with Maria's blessing!

If it were only so easy. He was afraid. A giant in the business world, a man often feared by others, and he was afraid to tell Peta that he loved her. And the reason why? Because he knew he couldn't handle it if she said that she didn't return his love.

The evening remained endless. Ten o'clock came, ten-thirty, eleven, eleven-thirty, and still no sign of Peta and Christos. Jealousy welled like a dam ready to burst. He knew he ought to go to bed, but he wanted to be here to see their faces, to look for any signs of emotional involvement. He needed to know.

And what if he did see it? What if he saw the light of love shining from Peta's eyes? Something he had never seen himself. What if he saw that particular soft radiance a woman had when she'd been well and truly made love to? How would he handle that?

With stoicism, he told himself. He'd give no hint that he was upset. But, he promised himself, he'd go all out to win Peta over, to convince her that he was the better man of the two. He'd tell her that he loved her; he'd get down on his knees if necessary and beg her to marry him. And that would be the most humbling experience of his whole life.

It was almost midnight before they returned. Andreas was pacing the hall when he heard the car and he would have liked nothing better than to stand and face them. But he couldn't do that. Instead he quickly took a seat in the living room, leaving the door open and the lights on so that they'd know he was in there. He picked up a book and pretended to be reading.

Peta had hoped that Andreas would be in bed. She'd had a most enjoyable evening with Christos. Once they'd established that there could be no romantic involvement they'd both let their hair down and set out to have a good time. He'd been excellent company, regaling her with tales of his childhood and his failed love affairs. By all accounts he was quite a ladies man and she could see why.

Both of these Papadakis brothers were gorgeous, with their dark Hellenic looks and strong masculine bodies. Andreas had the edge, though. He had a charisma that Christos didn't. Maybe it was his success, maybe it was because he was older, but, whatever, he was the one who would turn a girl's head first, and he was the one who had captured her heart.

'We didn't expect you to still be up,' said Christos now.

Andreas gave a lazy shrug and pushed himself to his feet. 'I wasn't particularly tired. Have you had a good time, you two?' His eyes rested on Peta as he spoke.

She knew that he had deliberately waited and was trying to assess whether she'd found Christos attractive, whether anything had gone on between them. She smiled warmly at Christos. 'We've had a wonderful time, haven't we?'

'Indeed.' He returned her look with warm affection. 'Am I glad you asked me to come and help you out over here, dear brother. And why you don't fancy Peta yourself I'll never know.'

Andreas's brows beetled into a scowl. 'I'm glad you enjoyed yourselves,' he grated. 'I think I'll go to bed.'

When he had gone Christos turned his lips down and looked at Peta with a questioning look in his eyes.

She shrugged.

'Methinks the man's jealous,' declared Christos.

'I think you're out of your mind,' she returned, 'and I'm going to bed, too. Thank you for a lovely evening.'

'Don't I get a goodnight kiss?'

She smiled slowly and put her arms about his shoulders. But when she leaned towards him all she did was kiss him on the cheek.

'That's cheating,' he growled.

'But it's all you're getting,' she said with a laugh. 'Goodnight, Christos.'

'Goodnight, beautiful lady.'

When Peta turned to leave the room she saw that Andreas had been watching them from the doorway. He'd turned immediately and marched along the corridor leading to their apartment, but he wouldn't have known that the kiss wasn't for real. Good, she thought with grim pleasure. That's the proof he needs that he means nothing to me.

And yet, as she slowly undressed and removed her make-up, as she cleaned her teeth and ran a brush through her hair, she couldn't help wishing that he hadn't seen.

She was not surprised when a few minutes later he tapped on the door and entered her room.

CHAPTER TWELVE

'DON'T tell me. You've come to find out whether I'm attracted to your brother.'

Peta's direct approach caused Andreas's eyes to flicker.

'If you have you're wasting your time, because however I feel towards Christos it's nothing to do with you,' she added firmly.

'So you do find him attractive?' Andreas crossed his arms over his chest and leaned back against the door, watching her intently through narrowed eyes. He was still in his shirt and trousers and it had obviously been his intent all along to come and interrogate her.

Peta's eyes flashed. 'Like I said, it's none of your business.'

'I intend to make it my business,' he countered firmly.

'Oh, yes, and how do you propose to do that?' She too folded her arms, wishing now that she hadn't got undressed. It was difficult trying to project an aloof and proud image wearing only a thin cotton nightie.

'I shall not go away until you give me some definite answers.'

Peta held his gaze for several long, heart-pumping seconds. Lord, he was magnificent. She wanted to haul him over to the bed and let him make love to her. She wanted him so badly that it hurt.

'What's wrong?'

'What do you mean?' she asked with a frown.

'Are you in pain?' He took a half-step towards her.

'No.' Not physical pain. And she cursed herself for letting her innermost feelings show.

'Then what's wrong?'

'You are what's wrong,' she retorted. 'Why won't you leave me alone?'

'Because I care about you.'

'Care!' retorted Peta crossly. 'You don't know the meaning of the word. You don't care about anyone. You didn't even care about your son until he was nearly taken from you.'

Andreas closed his eyes for a second, before saying quietly, 'Nikos means everything to me.'

'I've no doubt. But you never thought to show it. You never had time for him; business always came first.'

Her shot hit home. He winced. 'Not any longer.'

'So what are you going to do when I leave here? Get another nanny? Forget what you've just said? Leave Nikos to amuse himself all over again while you rake in the millions? You can't take it with you, Andreas. What's the point in devoting all your time to work at the expense of your son's happiness?'

'I've not come here to discuss my son.'

'No, you want to know what I think of Christos. Actually—' she allowed her face to soften into a dreamy smile '—he's a charmer. I wasn't sure at first, but the more I got to know him the more I discovered that I really like him. He's asked me out again.'

Andreas's eyes became glacially hard. 'And have you accepted?'

'Why, yes. He's such fun, and he's wonderful company. He makes me forget all my problems.'

'And what problems would those be?'

'As if you didn't know,' she shot back. 'The fact that my son was kidnapped. The fact that I can't get back into my own house. The fact that I'm forced to stay here with a man who wants an affair with me. Is that enough?'

Each barb shot home. She saw him wince. And his mouth grew grimmer and his eyes harder. 'Yes,' he said shortly. 'I can see that you do have problems. Perhaps I, as well as you, will be glad when you've gone.' And with that he spun on his heel and marched out.

Peta wanted to call him back, wanted to ask what he meant, but the door slammed and she hunched her shoulders and clenched her fists. Damn the man! Christos was wrong. Andreas wasn't jealous, not in the slightest. He was simply typically arrogant. Because he paid her wages he thought he owned her. Well, this was—

Her thoughts were interrupted by another knock on the door.

She wrenched it open. 'Andreas, if— Christos!'

'Are you all right?'

'Of course; why?'

'I saw my brother coming out with a face as black as thunder. What happened?'

'You'd better come in,' she said resignedly, and, once the door was closed, 'Like we arranged, I tried to pretend that I was falling for you.'

'And?'

She shook her head slightly. 'It got complicated. I said things I shouldn't have done. He ended up walking out on me. He doesn't love me, he just thinks he owns me. I'm not staying here any longer. I can't put up with any more of this.'

Christos frowned. 'Surely that's a bit hasty?'

'No, it's not. I never planned to stay once we got back.'

'Where will you go?'

'To my parents'.' It wasn't the ideal solution but what other choice had she? She didn't want to spend her hard-earned money on rented accommodation. Her mother and father would love having them for a few weeks. 'It means taking Ben out of school again but there's no alternative.'

'Are you sure you're doing the right thing? Why don't you let me have a word with Andreas? I could—'

'No!' cut in Peta in horror. 'I'll leave while you're both at work tomorrow. Don't say anything to your brother until you come back and find me gone. And even then don't tell him where I am. I'll make arrangements with Bess to have Nikos picked up from school.'

Christos shook his head. 'This isn't the answer.'

'Then what is?' she snapped.

'For you and Andreas to sit down and talk this thing over.'

'There's nothing to say. I'm not telling him I love him if that's what you want.' It would be the ultimate humiliation because, whatever Christos might think, she was absolutely certain that Andreas didn't love her.

'You're an idiot. A very beautiful one, but an idiot all the same.'

He was probably right. She would regret what she had done the moment she walked away. She would most likely tell herself that it would have been better to live with an Andreas who didn't love her rather than subject herself to a life without him.

She had little sleep that night. She lay awake, tossing her problem round and round in her mind. She was up early the next morning, getting the boys ready, having her breakfast with them in the kitchen, doing everything she could to avoid seeing Andreas.

But Andreas had no intention of avoiding her. As she

was leaving the kitchen, the boys having run on ahead, he caught her by the elbow and hustled her into his study. 'You and I have some talking to do.'

Peta feared that Christos had let her down, but Andreas's first words confirmed otherwise.

'What was Christos doing in your room last night?'

Peta felt like laughing—hysterically. She could have lied and said they'd made love, but that would get her nowhere. 'He came to see if I was all right. He saw you leave, heard you slam the door, saw the look on your face. He wondered what was going on.'

'So why didn't he ask me?' snarled Andreas.

'In the mood you were in? You'd have probably snapped his head off and told him it was none of his business.' Peta walked across to the window and pretended to look out at the immaculately manicured lawns.

'You're damn right, it's not,' came his harsh voice over her shoulder. 'What did you tell him?'

He'd moved so close that Peta could feel his breath on the back of her neck. And there was nowhere to go! Her own fault for putting herself into this position. 'That we'd had a few words.'

'He didn't ask what about?'

'Of course he asked. But I could hardly confess that his brother wanted a detailed report of the evening we'd spent together.'

'So what did you say?'

'Nothing much.' She wished he'd move. She wished he wouldn't stand so close. It was unnerving. It was churning her emotions. It was making her ask how could she possibly leave, feeling like this about him?

She continued to look out of the window, but when his hands touched her shoulders she jumped and went as tense as a high wire. He spun her to face him. He

looked deep into her eyes. And just when she thought
he was going to kiss her he let her go again and walked
to the other side of the room. But he still kept looking
at her.

'I wish I could meet the man who's done this to you,
Peta.'

She shot startled eyes in his direction. 'Done what?'
She had no idea what he was talking about.

'He must have hurt you very badly.'

She frowned then as realisation dawned. 'Are you
talking about Joe?'

'Of course I'm talking about Joe. And for you to still
be afraid of entering into a relationship nine years later
then he must have done a real hatchet job.'

Yes, it had made her wary and angry for a very long
time, but Joe was most definitely not the reason she was
holding Andreas at arm's length. Unknowingly, though,
he'd given her the perfect excuse. 'I was at a very vul-
nerable age,' she said quietly.

'He's a rat, and if I ever set eyes on him I'll kill him.'

There was such vehemence in his tone that Peta was
shocked. 'I hardly think it warrants that; it was a long
time ago.'

'And you're still suffering.'

Not to the extent he was suggesting, but she wasn't
going to admit that. If he knew the truth, if he knew that
he was the one who had managed to knock down her
defensive wall, she wouldn't have a minute's peace. 'I
really don't want to discuss this,' she said, and then
made a show of looking at her watch. 'I'd better check
the boys are ready for school. Are you taking Nikos or
shall I?'

'You do it,' he said brusquely. 'Christos and I need
to leave. We have an important meeting first thing.'

Yes, she thought, the same old pattern. He'd never change. He'd always put work before his son.

She didn't tell Ben her plans; she bundled them both into her car and as normal dropped Nikos off first. It was a few minutes before her son realised that they were heading back to the house. 'Have you forgotten something, Mummy?'

'No, darling, we're going down to Nanny and Grandad's for a few days. Won't that be fun?'

His little face lit up. 'I don't have to go to school?'

'No, you don't. But you're not getting out of it; I shall teach you myself, like I did before.'

'That's all right, I like you teaching me. Can Nikos come with us?'

Question followed question all the while she was packing and getting ready. Bess was sorry to see her go, sorry she wasn't getting on with Andreas.

'He knew I was going to leave, I simply didn't tell him when,' explained Peta.

'He'll be sad. You're the best thing that's happened to him in a long time.'

'If you say so,' said Peta, silently disagreeing. If she was the best thing he'd want more from her than an affair. As things stood he wanted a nanny for Nikos and a woman in his bed but no commitment, and as far as she was concerned it simply wasn't enough.

The drive to Cornwall didn't take very long. She hadn't told her parents to expect them and they were both stunned and delighted to see them. Freda and Doug James lived in a coastal village not far from Padstow and Ben was in his element, soon out of the house and down on the beach with his grandfather.

'How long are you staying?' asked her mother as she helped her unpack.

Peta shrugged. 'I don't know. I need a break. And then I'll look for a new job.'

'Why did you leave this one? I thought you liked it. And going to Greece as well. It sounds wonderful. I hope he paid you well?'

Peta nodded. 'Very well.' She had more money in the bank than she'd ever imagined. 'But it wasn't the idyll you imagine. Someone threatened to kidnap his son; that's why we fled.'

'Oh, my goodness! And you never told me,' shrieked her mother. 'You and Ben could have been in danger as well.'

Peta nodded and said as matter-of-factly as she could, so as not to alarm her mother further, 'As it turned out, Ben was kidnapped by mistake.'

Her mother's eyes rolled and she sat down on the edge of the bed. 'Tell me this isn't true.'

By the time Peta had finished explaining Freda James had still not come to terms with what had happened to her precious grandson. 'I don't blame you for leaving the man. It's not safe working for him.'

For the first time in her life Peta felt the need to confide in her mother. 'There's something more, Mum. The kidnapping's not the reason I left. I fell in love with Andreas.'

'I see.' Freda James's brows rose in surprise. 'It does complicate things. Am I right in presuming that he doesn't love you?'

Peta nodded. 'He's still hung up about his dead wife.'

'It's not easy, falling in love,' confided her parent. 'It ought to be, but too often there are complications. Oh, Peta, I've really missed you. It's been so long since you were last here.'

Peta nodded. 'Let's make up for it now.'

But Peta's thoughts were never far away from Andreas, and after lunch the following day, when Ben and her father had gone to the beach, she said, 'You know, Mum, Andreas is the first man I've ever truly loved. I know I thought I loved Joe, and was heartbroken when he dumped me, but, looking back, it wasn't love. He excited me, that was all.'

'And there's no chance of Andreas loving you in return?'

'Not one. I have to accept that he's not meant for me. He'd settle for an affair but I want more than that.'

'Of course you do, love. Best to push him right out of your mind. Ah, the phone, excuse me.'

Easier said than done, thought Peta as she left her mother to her phone call and joined Ben and her father. Andreas simply wouldn't go away.

When they got back to the house several happy if tiring hours later—Ben had run them ragged, racing around the beach and climbing over rocks—her mother seemed to be in an exceptionally good mood. She hummed and sang to herself as she gave Ben his supper, and afterwards, when he was in bed, she announced that she and Dad were going out.

'But you never go out at night,' Peta claimed with a frown.

'Doesn't mean to say we can't,' smiled her mum. 'I've left you a pie and some salad in the fridge. We shan't be late back. Enjoy yourself.'

What did she mean, enjoy herself? Time spent alone perhaps. That must be it. Peta wasn't hungry yet, so she settled herself outside in the back garden with a book and didn't hear the doorbell. She heard nothing until she sensed someone standing a few feet away. When she looked up and saw Andreas Papadakis her heart nearly jumped out of her chest. So who had told?

'Christos?' she enquired.

'No.'

'Bess?'

'That lady has given me one very good talking-to. I didn't know she had it in her.'

'And what exactly did she say?' Peta didn't invite him to sit. She didn't encourage him to take even a step further towards her.

'That she thought I had treated you despicably.'

Peta nodded, agreeing entirely.

'That she didn't blame you for walking out.'

'You left me no choice.'

'She told me I was a fool for not telling you that I loved you.'

'Huh!' she scorned. 'Why would you tell me that when we both know it's not true?' And why had Bess jumped to that conclusion?

'But it is true,' he answered quietly, his eyes darker now than she'd ever seen them, his face totally serious.

Peta's eyes widened. '*You* love *me*? You're joking, of course.'

'I'm not,' he said, shaking his head. 'I'm perfectly serious.'

This was more than she could take in. 'You've told my mother this? It was you on the phone earlier? It's why she's gone out? Hell, Andreas, you had no right.'

'I'm a desperate man,' he admitted, his expression wry.

'And what did my mother say about *my* feelings?' She urgently prayed that her parent hadn't given her away because she wasn't entirely sure that she believed Andreas. If he loved her, if he truly loved her, why couldn't he have said so? Why wait until she had run away and then decide? No, he still wanted her for his own selfish purposes.

'Precisely nothing,' he admitted. 'But she did agree that we ought to talk.' He closed the space between them in a few swift strides, dragging up a wrought-iron chair and positioning it so that he could sit facing her.

'You can talk all you like, it won't make any difference,' she said shortly. 'Words are easy.'

'If it's action you want then—'

'No!' She pulled back in distress as he tried to take her hands. 'Keep away from me, Andreas! I know what you're after. Why do you think I ran away?'

'And exactly what is it you think I'm after?' he asked, his mouth suddenly grim.

'An affair,' she thrust at him, top lip curling. 'It's all you've ever wanted. No commitment, just the use of my body—oh, and a babysitter for Nikos thrown in. Isn't that about right?'

'Maybe.'

'I knew I was right,' Peta claimed triumphantly.

'In the beginning.'

She frowned.

'I did desire you, fiercely. It turned into love without me even recognising it. The care you've shown for Nikos, as well as your own son, has awakened my responsibilities as a father and made me realise that I've loved you all along but tried desperately hard to bury it.'

'Because of Maria?'

He nodded. 'The time has come for me to let go.'

Peta was stunned. She didn't know what to say; she wasn't even sure whether she could believe him, even now, and he could see the doubt on her face.

'It's the truth, Peta.'

'So how did you trace me?'

'I overheard Christos telling Bess where you'd gone. All I had to do then was look on my itemised phone bill for your parents' number. Remember you rang them before we left for Greece?'

Peta closed her eyes. This was something she had never thought of.

'I know you don't return my love, Peta. But you like me, I think.' His brows rose, asking the question. 'And there's no denying the sexual attraction. We could work on it.' His eyes were such a dark brown that they appeared black, and they scanned her face closely, looking for some sign that she was weakening.

Peta felt a rush of emotion and could no longer hide her feelings. She reached out and took his hands into her own. 'Yes, Andreas, we can work on it,' she said softly, her heart beginning to race, her pulses quickening, and a soft heat enveloping her body.

'You really mean that?'

'I do.'

He stood up then and pulled her to her feet. 'May I hold you?'

She nodded, unable now to tear her eyes away from his. And her heart thumped as he urged her gently against the solid hardness of his body. He held her as though she was extremely fragile. 'This is more than I'd hoped for, Peta. I thought I'd have to work on you. I thought I'd have to woo you all over again.'

'It's more than I'd hoped for, too,' she admitted with a wry smile.

He looked down into her upturned face. 'What do you mean?'

'You have no idea how many times I've willed you

to fall in love with me and thought it would never happen. I thought you would never let go of Maria.'

He grew still. 'What are you saying?' And he seemed to be holding his breath as he waited for her answer.

'Can't you guess?'

He touched her chin and then stroked the backs of his fingers down her cheek, looking with almost childish wonder into her luminous blue eyes. 'I think you're saying that you love me, too.' And then he closed his eyes, as if to shut her out in case he was wrong, and she felt a tremor run through him.

'I do.' Her answer was little more than a whisper.

She heard the soft hiss of air as he exhaled, she felt the tension drain out of him, and like two lost souls who'd found each other in the wilderness they clung together, rocking and groaning, rocking and loving, pouring out their emotions in physical contact.

It was many long minutes before she lifted her head and he kissed her. Even then the kiss was gentle, tentative, experimental, as though he might frighten her away again if he asked for too much too soon.

'Tell me I'm not dreaming,' he whispered against her mouth.

'You're not dreaming,' she assured him huskily. 'I'm the one who's dreaming.'

'Oh, no! I love you, Peta. I love you very much. I shall tell you every day of my life. And if only I'd told you earlier then we wouldn't have wasted so much time.' His mouth captured hers again in a mind-drugging kiss that seemed to go on for ever.

When they finally managed to stop she was trembling so much that if he had let her go she would have fallen. He took her two hands into his and held them hard against his chest. She could feel his heart thudding. 'Will you marry me, Peta?' His gorgeous brown eyes held a burning light that threatened to consume her before the day was out.

It took her no more than a second to make up her mind, and her voice was a husky whisper. 'Yes.'

Andreas groaned, and his heart raced now like a mad thing beneath her hands. 'You wove your magic on me, Peta, from the first moment you walked into my office. Such a feisty female. You were entrancing. Don't ever change. And I promise I'll make you the happiest woman in the world.'

'Are you really over Maria?' It was a question she needed to ask.

He nodded. 'I love you in an entirely different way. It will be good between us. I'll never let you down the way Joe did.'

'I'm over Joe,' she told him with a wry smile. 'I used him as a buffer. I was scared of my feelings. I didn't believe that you'd ever love me, not the way I wanted to be loved, or the way I loved you.'

He frowned and looked at her closely. 'Are you saying that you've loved me for a long time?'

Peta gave a wry, guilty smile and nodded. 'Though, like you, I wasn't sure of it until after Ben's kidnapping. It's why I ran away.'

He swore loudly in Greek. 'Do your parents know how you feel about me?'

'My mother does,' she admitted. 'I expect she's told Dad.'

'I wondered why she was so ready to let me see you. Does anyone else know? Am I the last to hear? The one person who should be first?'

'It's your own fault,' she pointed out, though she smiled as she said it.

'I guess it is. But you haven't answered my question. How about Christos? Does he know? Were you talking about me on the night he took you out? I know he fancies you. Did you tell him he stood no chance because you loved me? Did you, Peta? Did you?'

He sounded angry and Peta didn't want to answer, but her expression must have given her away.

With a furious snarl Andreas let her go and put space between them, his eyes blazing accusation.

'He knew that you loved me,' she told him, 'and he wanted to talk to you but I wouldn't let him.'

'Damn! I can't believe I've been so blind, so foolish, so unbelievably ignorant.' He huffed out a sharp breath and paced the patio before coming once again to stand in front of her. 'My darling Peta, I have you to thank for showing me that there is still happiness to be found. My future beckons with all the brightness of a lodestar.'

'Oh, Andreas.' Tears welled and she clung to him, and to her surprise his eyes were suspiciously moist, too. 'This is the happiest day of my life.'

'We'll get married straight away,' he murmured between kisses. 'I'll get a special licence. I can't wait any longer.'

And if she was honest neither could Peta. She had finally found a man she could trust; a man who would never fail her; a man who would look after her for the rest of her life. What more could she ask?

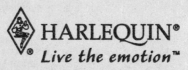

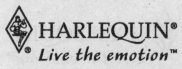

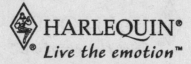

The world's bestselling romance series.

HARLEQUIN®
Presents
Seduction and Passion Guaranteed!

OUTBACK KNIGHTS
Marriage is their mission!

From bad boys—to powerful,
passionate protectors!

Three tycoons from the Outback
rescue their brides-to-be....

**Coming soon in Harlequin Presents:
Emma Darcy's exciting new trilogy**

Meet Ric, Mitch and Johnny—once three Outback bad
boys, now rich and powerful men. But these sexy city
tycoons must return to the Outback to face a new
challenge: claiming their women as their brides!

**MAY 2004: THE OUTBACK MARRIAGE RANSOM #2391
JULY 2004: THE OUTBACK WEDDING TAKEOVER #2403
NOVEMBER 2004: THE OUTBACK BRIDAL RESCUE #2427**

*"Emma Darcy delivers a spicy love story...
a fiery conflict and a hot sensuality."*
—Romantic Times

Available wherever Harlequin books are sold.

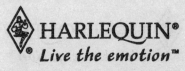

HARLEQUIN®
Live the emotion™

Visit us at www.eHarlequin.com   HPEDARCY

The world's bestselling romance series.

HARLEQUIN®
Presents~

Seduction and Passion Guaranteed!

MILLIONAIRE MARRIAGES

When the million-dollar question is "Will you marry me?"

Coming Soon in Harlequin Presents...
An exciting duet by talented author

Sandra Field

Don't miss...

May 2004: The Millionaire's Marriage Demand #2395
Julie Renshaw is shocked when Travis Strathern makes an outrageous demand: marriage! She is overwhelmingly attracted to him—but is she ready to marry him for convenience? Travis is used to getting his own way—but Julie makes certain he won't this time...unless their marriage is based on love as well as passion....

June 2004: The Tycoon's Virgin Bride #2401
One night Jenessa's secret infatuation with tycoon Bryce Laribee turned to passion—but the moment he discovered she was a virgin he walked out! Twelve years later, the attraction between them is just as mind-blowing, and Bryce is determined to finish what they started. But Jenessa has a secret or two....

Available wherever Harlequin books are sold.

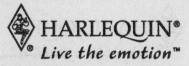

HARLEQUIN®
Live the emotion™

Visit us at www.eHarlequin.com

HPMILMAR